THE TABLE BY THE WINDOW

and other stories

CALDWELL IDAHO WRITERS GROUP
ANTHOLOGY Vol. 1

ISBN: 978-1-7335720-7-1

This is a work of fiction and nonfiction. Any references to historical events, real people, or real places are used fictitiously unless otherwise stated.

Front cover image by Alyssa Cumpton
Book design by Angela Matlashevsky

First printing edition 2020

Table of Contents

Foreword

What does a collection of horror, comedy, science fiction, true-life, and modern-day western stories have in common? They are the collective effort of the Caldwell Idaho Writers Group and are published as the book you are now holding in your hand – *The Table by the Window*.

The Table by the Window is the first book by this group of seasoned and aspiring Idaho writers, and runs the gamut from the inspirational to the macabre. Featured inside are stories by Michael T. Smith, an acclaimed local writer frequently featured in the *Chicken Soup of the Soul* series; the title story *The Table by the Window* by Neil James, a popular western author who specializes in tales of the Owyhee Mountains; fantasy and sci-fi stories by brother and sister team S.C. Fantozzi and Andrew Majors; a hilarious comedic tale of vengeful bees by area realtor Elinor Dolore; a humorous poem penned by the book's designer (and local artist extraordinaire) Angela Matlashevsky; an essay on the benefit of serendipitous travel by Steve Prager; coming of age stories by fantasy writer Merri Halma; and finally, a trove of stories and poems ranging from a mother's love to decapitation by co-chair Stacia Perry, writing as SueDean Morris.

So sit back and enjoy. There is something for everyone in this wonderful anthology. And when you're finished, we hope you'll agree that Idaho is famous for something besides potatoes!

Happy reading!
Caldwell Idaho Writers Group

The Table by the Window

Warm Fuzzies

Stories to make
you smile.

NEIL JAMES has, since his childhood, spent his happiest days exploring the backcountry of the fabled Owyhee Mountains of Southwestern Idaho. His family roots in these mountains reaches back to 1863 when his great grandfather arrived in search of gold and started a family tree of five generations loving the same area.

The Table by the Window is one of the short stories in a forthcoming collection of short essays paying tribute to the kind of people who still live and cherish the life of mining and ranching areas of mountainous Idaho.

THE TABLE BY THE WINDOW

Neil James

Clyde Collins sat at the establishment's old counter and surveyed each table. The café wasn't full, maybe half full, and there were at least three empty tables. It was a slight irritation that the one table next to the window was occupied. Clyde sat at that table every morning for two to three hours: he had done this for more than nine years. Clyde tried not to stare at the young couple who sat there. They had finished their omelets, hash browns and toast over 10 minutes ago. They had already paid their bill and the tip money was on the table. June had cleared away the dishes leaving only their two coffee cups. He tried not to stare at the table. He didn't want to make them feel uncomfortable but his stress level was building as he waited for them to stand up and walk out. He looked at the clock that hung above the service window next to the white board that listed the day's pies. 9:20! The bus could be rolling in at any second.

June walked over to him and again asked if she couldn't at least get him a cup of coffee.

"Nah, no thanks, Honey. I'll just wait for my table. Shouldn't be all that long now."

June gave him an understanding nod and, picking up two coffee pots, began making the rounds to refill cups. One pot held regular and the other decaf. Clyde watched her as she went from customer to customer and finally approached *his* table. He was relieved to see the woman shake her head with a smile but concerned when he saw the man indicate about an inch. June slopped in a small amount of decaf without spilling a drop, smiled, said something Clyde couldn't catch and then moved on.

The table was special. It was at that table where she told him that she was leaving him for good. He had thought that he was just taking her to the bus stop so she could go visit her sister in Yakima. While they were waiting for the bus she broke the news to him. He had taken it well at the time because she had told him she was leaving before. She had always relented and come back within a few days. He was sure this time would be no different. He had just nodded his understanding and told her he would be sitting right here at this table when she came back.

That had been 9 years ago. Although she had come back to town several times over the years for weddings, funerals and a couple other special occasions, she had always stayed with friends and left again when the event was finished. The last time had been three years ago. It had been his mother's funeral. Katherine had even given him a quick hug at the church.

He had managed a shaky "Thanks, Kat."

"How you holding up?" she asked.

"Oh, I'm fine Kat. Just waitin' for you to come home."

As she sadly shook her head, and turned away, he thought he saw a hint of a tear. Of course, it could have been for his mother, she and Kat had been very close at one time, but he preferred to think it was for him. Maybe there was no tear at all. Maybe he just wished it had been there. He had a hard time remembering now.

He thought he might get a chance to talk with her later at the memorial. But she hadn't attended. The hug was the last time he had seen her. Still, his hope never wavered. She still sent Christmas cards and birthday cards each year. They were somewhat generic but still, it showed she was still thinking of him.

Most important to Clyde was the fact that not once, in all these years, had she ever uttered the divorce word. She was still his wife and he was still her husband.

About a year after she left, he had called to ask when she was coming home. It was then that she had told him that she would always love him but she could not live with the man he had become. He had tried to tell her how he was better now but somehow the words just didn't work right. She had said he probably shouldn't call anymore because it was too painful for both of them. He had honored that request.

He relived all of this every morning. He watched through the window every morning while the infrequent passenger stepped from the bus. He felt his heart fall every time the bus pulled away and didn't leave her standing there. It had been that way for 9 years.

He had been a long haul truck driver and she had worked in the hardware store across the street from The Bus Stop Café where he now waited for his table. They had met late in life. Their marriage had been a good one in his mind. Oh, she had been critical of his drinking binges but most of his truck driving buddies had a beer now and then. Many had addictions to uppers to keep them awake. He had never done that and thought she should give him a little credit for that at least.

When he did drink too much he was never obnoxious or threatening to her. In fact, quite the opposite. He became overly happy and sometimes way too amorous. She was rarely in the mood for this drunken attention and often rejected his advances. He would just shrug his shoulders and head into the bedroom where he would pass out. In the mornings after these binges, he would wake up in his same clothes and she would be on the couch.

The binges that were unknown to either of them in the first couple years of marriage had started when he wrecked his eighteen-wheeler and found that his limited insurance wouldn't come close to replacing it with anything useable. He was forced to drive for some of the larger carriers. To Clyde, this was embarrassing. A lot of his pride had left him and he started drinking a bit when he was off the road. His income had been cut in half and he felt less than the man he had been. Within another year he was often drunk for days at a time. Even when drunk, he was always respectful to all who encountered him and especially to Kat. He began to get drunk when he had lay overs away from home and would go for two or three days without calling her, leaving her to wonder if he was alive or dead. He would increasingly fail to pick up loads and began to lose the jobs he had driving.

Fed up with these episodes, Kat had warned him that no matter how much she loved him, she just couldn't continue living like that. Out of frustration, she had left for days at a time to visit her parents or her sister. He would always promise to straighten up if she would just come back. She always had and, for a few weeks, things would be good again. And, when things were good, they were very good. Then, something would happen and he would fall back to the bottle again. The story repeated itself for years until finally, after an especially scary week of not knowing where he was, she had reached her breaking point. She arranged to stay with her sister until she could decide what to do.

The next day, after Clyde had finally called her to apologize and say he would be home the next day, she loaded up her clothes and her personal items and put it on the bus to her sister. When Clyde got home early the next morning she asked him to take her to The Bus Stop Cafe. Kat told him she needed to get away for a while and was going to her sister's for a visit. Once they were in the café, at the table by the front window, she told him the truth.

She was not coming back.

He had moved to the little town of Craters, Oregon when he was 35. He had driven through it a hundred times on runs to California. When his first wife had died in a car crash he had been completely lost. Slowly, he started to recover but every place he looked in Boise, where they had lived, reminded him of her. He decided to sell their little house and move someplace completely different. Something about the little cow town of Craters felt good. He bought a small acreage on the outskirts and bought a pair of cowboy boots and a genuine Stetson hat. He chose a flat brim like the ones in pictures he had seen of long ago. He had donated all of his furniture from the Boise place and slowly started furnishing his new home.

He started with a single size bed: that replaced the big queen size of his last home. He had found the folks in town to be friendly and with no need to have him rehash his past. After several years he had settled into his routine and was fairly happy, but lonely.

Then he met Kat.

Kat had grown up on a cattle ranch just outside of Craters and after going to college for two years decided she wanted to come back home. She, too, had lost her first spouse. They had a rather strange arrangement in that she lived on the ranch in her parents' house and he lived at their home in Nampa. He owned and operated a pharmacy there and went to the ranch most weekends. Although they had no children, their marriage had otherwise been a happy one.

He had been rounding up cattle on a long weekend at the ranch when his horse stumbled after stepping in a gopher hole as he chased an errant steer. Not being an experienced rider, her husband was tossed from the saddle onto the horse's neck. At this, the horse veered sharply to the left and the man was thrown to the ground. He landed on a sharp rock that sent a broken rib into his lungs. By the time they were able to get him out of the hills to the hospital two hours later, his lungs had filled with blood and he died within another half hour.

Kat sold their home and had a double-wide, manufactured home delivered to a site a couple hundred feet from her parent's house on the ranch. It was only about twenty minutes to town when the weather was favorable and more out of boredom than need, Kat took a job at the hardware store owned by an old family friend.

Four years later her parents sold the ranch to the neighbor and retired to Arizona. They paid Kat a substantial sum out of the proceeds and she paid a token rent for room and board to the folks that owned the hardware store. She occupied a small apartment located above the store. She had lived there about six months when one of the regular patrons, Clyde, got up the nerve to ask her if she'd have supper with him the following Saturday night. She was lonely and said yes.

The relationship developed slowly, the occasional lunch or supper when Clyde had a day or two off the road. The months went by like that until one day she took a day trip with him to Boise and back when he was finishing up a delivery from California. They laughed a lot and sat up on his porch that night until they realized it was past midnight. He walked her home and she gave him a hug, the first sign of real affection shown by either of them. Neither knew if they were over their losses and were nervous about allowing those kind of feelings again.

It was Clyde that finally decided to move forward. He had known for a long time that he loved Kat but only recently realized that he was *in love* with her. On a moonlit night in September they strolled along the only real business street in town, hand in hand, as they greeted others doing the same thing. Clyde suggested they get a couple of cokes to sip on as they walked. They drifted back to his pickup at the city park. He held both cokes and asked Kat to reach into his jacket pocket for the keys. Instead of keys she pulled out a little black box.

"Well, what in the world is that?" grinned Clyde.

"It was in *your* pocket, not mine. How would I know?"

"Well, why don't you open it and see? Here, turn toward the street light so we can see inside."

She turned away from him toward the light. When she
opened it and saw the little engagement ring she gasped
and turned back toward Clyde. He was on one knee and
grinning at her like he had just won the lottery.

"Well, so what do you think? Are you willing to wear
that thing for about a hundred years?"

The bus was scheduled to be in at 10:00 A.M. each and
every morning. It was a joke with everyone in Craters. It
was common knowledge that the *10:00 A.M.* written on
the schedule should have had a *+/- one hour* attached to it.
If the bus arrived early it would leave promptly at ten
o'clock. If it arrived late, it would leave as soon as the
driver could fill his insulated cup with coffee and go to the
bathroom. The bus had a toilet onboard so he never waited
for passengers to do anything more than stretch their legs
while he was in The Bus Stop Café.

June and Rose, the other waitress who arrived about
10:00 to help out for lunch, both liked it when it came in
early. On those occasions, the patrons often came in to eat
something. It usually meant at least ten or fifteen dollars
more in the day's tips. Carl Triston, the crusty old geezer
that owned the place and did the cooking, always grum-
bled about the extra work but didn't seem to mind the
added income.

The menu at The Bus Stop was simple: breakfast consisted of choices of two types of omelets (ham and cheese or bacon and cheese). The other choices were scrambled eggs or once over eggs. All came with sourdough hot cakes or toast and a huge pile of hash browns. The patron could choose bacon or ham as a side with their eggs. Whatever the choice, the price was the same for all.

The breakfast menu was printed on the back side of postcards. The front side showed Craters' main street as it appeared in 1892. Ten years ago, a salesman from Boise had stopped in and convinced Carl to buy a sampling of the menus. Somehow, the order of fifty had turned into an order of five thousand. Carl had refused to pay for more than fifty and the salesman had never come back to pick up the extras. After a year, Carl had started using those, too. Now, customers were welcome to take the things with them if they so desired.

Lunch was even less complicated and no menu had ever been created for lunch. First time customers were usually confused when they were only asked what they wanted to drink and were they here for lunch. If they said "yes" to the lunch question, their waitress would walk back toward the service window and call out the number of people wanting lunch. Carl would shift the unlit cigar from one side of his mouth to the other and toss the appropriate number of patties onto the grill.

Without ever seeing a menu or ordering anything, after a few minutes, the eaters were served a huge plate of fries topped with an oversized bun that supported a big patty topped with a thick slice of melted, sharp cheddar cheese.

Slices of onion, lettuce and pickle were tucked to one side of the plate. Beside the burger plate a divided, oblong bowl was placed. One side of this strange looking bowl contained a serving of cottage cheese and the other side held chunks of unsweetened fruit cocktail. For twenty five years, June and Rose had been reciting the same explanation. The fruit was to cleanse the pallet in order to fully experience the mouthwatering taste of the locally grown ground beef. It should be eaten first.

The first day after Kat left town, the first day after she left Clyde, was a Saturday. Just before nine o'clock, Clyde Collins walked through the door, gave a wave to June and settled into a chair at the table by the front window. June brought him a cup of coffee and asked if he wanted breakfast. He chuckled and said that he might as well; no telling when the bus would roll in. She brought him his usual ham and cheese omelet and ask who he was waiting for.

"Oh, Kat got this wild hair about going to visit her sister. I expect her back today though."

He was a bit disappointed when she didn't show up but not too surprised. After all, she had stayed away for five days that one time. That was a couple years back.

Yesterday afternoon, he had called the trucking outfit and told them he had some business to take care of and couldn't take any loads for a week or so and they were understanding. Truth was, as much as they liked Clyde, after this last episode they had already decided to use him only as a backup driver.

He wanted to be here, at this table, when Kat got off the bus. That might be tomorrow or the next day or even next week. Besides, he wanted a few days to get over the sluggishness he was feeling from this last binge. He had made up his mind that he would never take another drink. Never! This time, when Kat returned, she would find the man she had married and that man would never again let her down.

At 8:45 Sunday morning he again sat down at the window table to wait. Becky, the Sunday waitress, asked if he wanted breakfast as she set the steaming cup of coffee in front of him. He said yes and was a bit amused that he had to tell her what he wanted. He was nearly always home on weekends and it was a ritual for him and Kat to have breakfast here on Sunday mornings. Becky had taken the same order from him almost every Sunday morning for the past six years. She always remembered what Kat wanted but never once had she failed to ask what he would have. Becky never smiled at him or gave any indication of recognition. On the other hand, she and Kat would talk at length about everything under the sun.

Oh well, what the heck? Kat would probably get off the bus today and that would make everything OK again.

By the time the following Friday came and went, the whole town knew that Katherine Collins had finally walked away from Clyde for good. Everybody knew both of them well and few if any held any animosity toward Clyde. He was, they nearly all agreed, a very good man when he was sober and that was most of the time. Even when they saw him drunk, they nearly all agreed he was always fun to be around. But, they nearly all agreed, Kat had endured his binges way beyond what anyone could expect and it was way past time for her to move on to a better life. Clyde, they agreed, should be treated well and with respect. After all, when he was sober, he was a very good man.

Clyde never again drove a long haul eighteen wheeler. He just couldn't manage the thought of missing the bus that would bring Kat back to him. He had no trouble picking up local hauls through the many contacts he had. After all, when Clyde was sober, he was very dependable. And now-a-days he was always sober. He drove cattle truck, water truck, delivery truck, gravel truck and anything else offered. He was busy most all the time. The only requirement, as all understood, was that he was not available until the bus left The Bus Stop Café each day.

The days had turned to weeks, the weeks to months and then years. Clyde had not once touched a drink of alcohol since the day Kat left. Oh, he had had his challenges. Sometimes on Saturday nights he would sit on his porch where they had spent so many summer evenings laughing and talking. She would sip her wine and he would nurse a Coors. On some of these lonely nights he felt an urge to drink. One time, about six months after she had taken the bus, he actually went to the liquor store and bought a fifth of rye. He brought it back to the porch and took the cap off. He started to put it up to his mouth when he got a healthy whiff of the stuff. All of the hurt in her face from all those times before came sweeping into his mind. Instead of taking that drink, he took the empty bottle into the house and placed it where the booze had always been kept. From that time forward, whenever the temptation to drink came to him, he would walk to the empty bottle, remove the cap and take a deep inhale of the remaining fumes. That would do it. He'd replace the cap and put the bottle down and walk away.

Clyde's morning ritual was unchanged. He would get up and take a shower. Get dressed. Make the bed to perfection using the decorative pillows that Kat had so liked. He would survey the entire house to make sure everything was just the way she liked it. He kept the few dishes he used washed and put away. He mopped the floors at least twice a week and more if needed. The entire property was kept in immaculate condition. After all, he reasoned, today could be the day that she comes home.

So, here sat Clyde, as he had every day for the past nine plus years, waiting for his chance to get his place at the table by the window. The young couple finally stood up and made their way out the door. Clyde quickly gathered his hat and yesterday's newspaper and strode to the table. June came over with a big smile and brought him a cup and poured his coffee.

"Breakfast Clyde?"

"Why, of course, June! Do I look like I'm the dieting type?"

They both laughed and Clyde took his first look at the paper. It was the weekly edition put out by a newspaper from a farming community across the Idaho border about 60 miles away. Since it was the only paper remotely close to Craters, it often carried stories about it, too. He read with interest about the rising price of cattle. He didn't own any and never had, but the economy of Craters lived and died with the price of cattle. It was ranching, and only ranching, that supported the entire area. If he were to continue to get well paid for driving trucks belonging to local businesses and ranchers and the county, it would be because the price of cattle was holding its own.

It's always a guessing game for ranchers. Some years bring the snow high in the mountains during the long winters. With the spring thaw, the runoff from the snow begins. In those years the water runs high as it tumbles down the gullies and washes to the creeks and rivers below. In those years, if the winter isn't too cold, *cold* as in *kill the cattle in the field cold*, the hay crops and grass for grazing will be good. But the flip side of the weather coin is always on the ranchers' minds as well. Those are the drought years, the years when winter snowfall is minimal and the creeks run low or dry by mid-summer. In those years, and they often run for several years in a row, ranchers can't grow enough hay and the grazing grass runs out early. As a result, the owners are forced to buy hay from the valley at high prices to feed their stock. Between the high cost of that hay, and the extra cost of getting it delivered, the profits are easily eaten up. A few years of drought can break a rancher that is running tight to begin with.

The morning had been cool for late August but welcome. Southeastern Oregon is high desert with a distinct steppe climate. Most of the lower valleys are still over 2,000 feet in elevation. The higher valleys, like that where Craters is found, is over 4,000 feet above sea level. Craters' valley is surrounded by mountains looming an additional 4,000 feet above the town. Up high, in the high country, the air is usually crisp and cooler. Below, at Craters, its elevation does little to stem the heat. It's often over 90 degrees in August. Clyde had walked the half mile from his place to The Bus Stop, humming as he walked and deeply breathing in the freshness of the morning air. As usual, the few parking places around the place were occupied with pickup trucks and the occasional city rig. Clyde had surveyed the parked vehicles with only a passing interest. He didn't see any that he recognized. A couple with California plates: that wasn't unusual. Highway 95, which ran through Craters, was a main route between Idaho and California. Folks coming from the south hadn't had a real place to stop in well over a hundred miles. Like Clyde had often done decades earlier, long haul truck drivers often stopped for a break as well. He casually noted an Idaho plate and had a bit more interest when he saw a Washington State tag. Since he knew Kat still lived in Washington State near her sister, he always felt a twinge when he saw a Washington car. He noted the outline of someone sitting in the car but paid little attention. He walked into the café and noted the time on the clock: about 8:55. He was a little later than normal but didn't worry. The bus had never been earlier than ten after nine. He stepped through the door and turned to his right and the table by the front window. He stopped short as the startled couple sitting there looked up at him.

"Oops, sorry folks. My mistake."

He tipped his hat and hurried over to the counter where he took a stool.

Now that they had left and he had his table, and June had brought his breakfast and refilled his coffee cup, he was relaxed and watched through the window for the bus. It would come in from the Idaho side. After stopping here, it would continue to Nevada and then California as it first passed through this corner of Oregon.

As he had done every day, he would feel himself stiffen as he saw it come around the corner and pull to a stop. He would hear the air release from the brakes and the doors would open and the disembarking passengers, if any there were, would gingerly step off and stretch after the long ride. He would expectantly look for her and then slump a bit when she wasn't there. He really knew that she might never come back. He wasn't crazy. At least he didn't think he was. It was just that, well, what if she did come back one day and he wasn't there at their table where he said he would be? For nine years that thought alone had kept him coming in every day.

He had not even considered another woman over these years. For one thing, he knew he could never feel that way again. She had been, and still was, the *one*. They were still married! He didn't know if he could survive if she ever ended that.

He was considering that as he saw the bus come around the corner. Only the driver got off. It was already after ten and within five minutes the driver, fresh coffee in hand, climbed back in and closed the door. The big engine roared and the silver beast slowly rolled away. He hadn't seen another vehicle pull into the parking area just outside but he heard a car door close. In the back of his mind he knew it had to be the person in the Washington car that he had noticed earlier. He was still re-playing the bus pulling away and thought nothing beyond that.

As usual, he gave the slightest of shrugs and happened to glance to where June was standing behind the counter. She was grinning at him. He didn't understand. He gave her a confused half smile and looked back down at his barely touched breakfast. He heard the café door open and was vaguely aware that someone had come in. He didn't sense the person standing by his table until he heard her voice.

"Hey truck driver, how about sharing your breakfast with your wife?"

ELINOR DOLORE lives in the Treasure Valley of Idaho with her retired husband and two dogs. Time spent with family, four grown kids and five grandkids, is one of best parts of her life along with reading, gardening, hiking and good friends.

What can happen when a
Realtor meets with clients
to look for property?

A Stinging Afternoon

Elinor Dolore

I have had many interesting experiences in my years of working as a Realtor. One particular incident that has stayed in my mind happened at least ten years ago. Whenever it pops up a smile begins to spread across my face and I can't help laughing out loud. The picture of that particular day of showing property has never left my memory.

I was working with a husband and wife who resided in a small town. They loved and owned horses but had to board them since they lacked adequate space in their sub-urban subdivision, and we were on a mission to find them acreage where they could live and share their space with the horses that meant so much to them. This type of property can be difficult to find and we had searched for two weeks so far. The search had taken us to many rural areas of the valley. My clients were getting anxious and worried that we might not find the perfect spot.

On a bright and sunny Saturday I set out once again with the husband, minus his wife this time but with his excited dog in tow. I led the way with my client following in his own car. We both had high hopes for the property we were going to peruse in a small town to the north. The hunt had taken us to quite a few acreages but none of them had the size, topography, or magic my clients were looking for in a forever-with-horses happy ending.

We finally arrived at our destination and the three of us exited our vehicles. What a breathtaking view we encountered! To the Northeast were apple and cherry orchards as far as our eyes could see. To the south of the land was a tall ridge with gray boulders perched precariously in odd spots, and grasses and bushes covering the hillside. It looked as if wildflowers would be in bloom soon and there were a few lofty trees getting ready to burst forth with soothing shade for the all that wandered that striking ridge. On the very top was the two-lane highway that had brought us to the little town and this piece of property. I looked up and saw cars following the winding road on its way down into the beautiful valley.

We were ready to begin the exploration. I was dressed in my walk-the-land Realtor outfit and my client had his walking boots and protective soft-brimmed hat for protection from the flying things that were out and about now and from any sunshine that would hopefully warm up the chilly, early spring day. The dog was just eager to get the hike underway as he leaped and bounded around his human. The size of the property was almost eleven acres. We were going to walk the entire piece to make sure there was a great spot to build a home and another good area for a barn and other needed structures. My clients were also very concerned about old apple wood that might be lying around because apple trees had once filled this acreage with their scented blossoms and luscious fruit, and horses, he told me, love apple wood but it can make them very sick and possibly kill them. The splinters could lodge in their stomachs and cause a lot of damage. That's why as we walked his head was down most of the time searching the ground for any sign of danger.

By this time our exploring had taken us a long ways from the cars. We were searching and talking quite a bit but not paying much attention to anything outside of the promising possibilities of this great piece of land. I looked up to observe the beautiful day and view when I noticed the dog was a good distance from our spot. He seemed to be acting very exuberant as he jumped up and down, twisting his head farther around than seemed possible even for a dog. I turned to my client who was very absorbed in a stick poking out of the ground by his feet. I asked him if this was normal behavior for his dog. He glanced at me and then the dog and shrugged a little as he looked back down at the stick. He assured me that his dog was a little goofy sometimes but just having a great day.

I'm sure that people who love their animals know them well so I turned away from the dog and started to ask my client if the stick was the feared apple wood. Before he could answer, a yelp sounded that must have been heard at the top of the ridge. We looked at the dog and saw that his behavior was well beyond exuberant and goofy; he was highly agitated. We ran towards the traumatized or possessed animal and as soon as we came close a scream erupted from my client's mouth that sent shivers down my spine. As soon as his scream was loosened and let go, the word "BEES!" came out with extreme venom (I know). I was really startled but still did not comprehend the gravity of the situation. In that same second he had started running towards the car and waving his soft-brimmed hat erratically. The dog started running towards him so I started running too, yelling "What's wrong?"

"Bees!" he shouted while running and trying to explain without pitching headfirst into the dirt. "The dog must have kicked up a nest!" his trailing voice shouted. That made me run faster because I could actually see some angry buzzing bees, hornets or wasps. I wasn't sure which they were at that point and it didn't really matter. I had long hair and as I ran my hands were swatting at the air all around me and at my head. Suddenly I felt the pain of a sharp stinger entering my scalp. Have you ever tried extracting bees from wild, flying, long hair? It's impossible.

By now my client was close to his car and the dog seemed to have settled down and was wagging his tail. My client however was still in panic mode. I made it to his car completely out of breath and trying to get the question "What's wrong?" to come forth again. He looked at me with sheer terror in his eyes and managed to inform me he was deathly allergic to bees! He was scrambling to open his EpiPen kit and save his life. Luckily, as soon as he had the kit in his grasp and opened, he calmed down and realized he hadn't even been stung! The dog was fine too and even had that look on his face that dogs get when they don't understand why the fun has stopped.

On the other hand, I had a scalp on fire and was in extreme pain. My client noticed then that I had been stung and he felt terrible. He was very worried that I was allergic to bees and he wanted to use the EpiPen on me. I assured him that I had been stung many times in my life and all without incident of allergic reactions. He did insist that I take some Benadryl from the kit. I agreed that it might be a good idea since I had to drive about thirty-five miles to my house. We said our goodbyes and he promised to follow me until he had to turn in the direction that would take him home.

I finally made it safely home, still in great pain and feeling a slight dizziness, but I recovered quickly and that evening while I was sitting on the couch I recounted to my husband the events of the day. As I was telling him the story I started laughing at the mental picture in my mind of the three of us with arms and hat flying and feet running as fast as they could go. I pictured the people in their cars on top of the ridge looking down onto the beautiful, bucolic scene and witnessing two people and a dog acting like wild, crazy people in some kind of cult or something.

Picturing it through their eyes makes me laugh even harder. It must have been a hilarious sight!

The thing is, I'm not usually afraid of bees and I was the only one that got stung! My clients did end up purchasing the property and really love their life there. For me it was another real estate adventure in a long list of adventures that make being a Realtor so fun.

A poem detailing a mother's love
and fears about motherhood.

I Will Love You Forever ♥

SueDean Morris

Nine months, about 243 days,
　　　is how long I knew about you before I met you.
I was scared, nervous, and excited to meet you.
I wondered what you would be like.
　　　I imagined what you would look like.
Even then I couldn't imagine my life without you in it.
You made me realize what was really important.

In the beginning, I threw up everything you didn't like.
　　　My back hurt.

I couldn't get comfortable.
I cried at every little thing.
        I dreamt the strangest dreams.
And yet, your somersaults and kicks
        always made me smile.

The day you were born was the happiest day of my life.
The pain I felt after the epidural wore off was worth
        hearing you coo.
The scar from hip to hip was worth seeing your beautiful
        brown eyes.
The lack of sleep was worth holding you close,
        and kissing your head.

As you got older, your every accomplishment
        makes me so proud.
I'm sure by now people are tired of hearing about you.
About how much you have grown.
        About how much you have learned.
About what funny thing you have done today.
About your newest quirk,
        or your newest drawing.
The thing is, I don't care if people are tired of hearing
        about you.
I am your biggest fan, and you are my life.

♥

You may not know this, but you made my life brighter.
You have made my life more exciting.
    You have given me new purpose.
I can see your eyes watching, waiting to copy.
It is scary to know that I have you watching.
Each morning the show starts
    and each night the curtain falls.
And there you are in the front row watching.
You will see all my accomplishments,
    and all my failures.
You will see all of the mistakes I make, and I worry that
    you will repeat them.

♥

I would live with every discomfort and every ache
    to have you.
We will fight.
    We will argue.
No matter what I want you to remember.
You are my daughter, and I am your mother.
And no matter what I will love you
    forever.

Take a Picture of This

S.C. Fantozzi

Abby Marcus couldn't remember the last time she'd felt the dirt under her feet. The scent of sage bloomed around her, stirred by her feeble movements as she gingerly worked her way up the gentle slope. The going was slow, hampered by her aching knees and labored breaths. One slipper-clad foot fought for purchase against the cinder-laden soil and the resulting cascade of stone sent a rabbit bolting from behind a pile of rocks. She felt the edge of her paper thin lips tip up into a smile as the cotton tail disappeared into the brush.

It was so good to be out.

She didn't bother looking back as she resumed her slow trudge up the incline, scraggly twigs and bits of downy brome catching in her loose sweatpants. There was nothing behind her that she wanted to see, the time there having long ago become stale and predictable, each day ending with a lingering sense that she was missing some part of her soul.

The sky was clear, a brilliant blue in the fading autumn sun. Night would fall soon enough, but for the moment the breeze was crisp and she was free. The ache in her back nudged at her again, but she beat back the pain. There wasn't much time.

If she'd been able to see her reflection in the tawny soil, she'd have been met by the lidded eyes of an old woman, one who'd seen more than her share of strife and heartache. Her hair had been white for nearly a decade, though it still fell in a curving braid between her bony shoulder blades. Joints swollen with arthritis didn't move with the grace they once had, and her mind had begun to slip, more and more of her memories stolen away as her will waged an endless battle against time.

Old and feeble though she was, Abby had managed to hold onto a single spark of defiance, the same spark that had saved her life on more than one occasion.

It had taken some work, and more than a little planning, but lifting a set of keys from one of her caretakers had rolled her aching bones into motion. Hotwiring a car had come back to her as naturally as breathing, the thought of giving up never once crossing her mind. She'd piloted the old Chevy out into the desert without hesitation, driving over ruts and bumps until she couldn't have made it back home even if she wanted.

Undoubtedly, the staff at the care home where she'd spent the last three years were frantically searching, desperate to figure out how a ninety year old, senile woman had managed to escape their grasp. They were honest people who'd treated her well enough, and though she couldn't help but feel a slight twinge of guilt, the feeling was quickly smothered by the joy of being free.

The small hill she was hiking up was a cobble of stone and sage, the deep rusty rocks jutting up from sandy earth like islands adrift in a desert sea. A cicada sang underfoot and she managed another choked breath, heart pumping wildly as she asked it for more than it could give, desperate to reach the top.

The ground that suddenly rushed up to impact her knees was harder than she remembered, bruising paper-thin skin even through sweats. Hands no longer accustomed to the abrasiveness of dirt caught her as she lurched forward, the mountains far off in the distance wincing in sympathy as she felt blood rush to her palms, bursting forth in dots and streaks.

Abby didn't care, even as pain assaulted her. For the first time in years, she felt alive, humming out her joy in a nameless tune.

The desert called still, urging her on, the sagebrush singing along with the faint current of air that brushed across her neck like a caress. The scent of salt and stone and something she'd never managed to describe coiled around her, a pleasant sensation that nearly brought tears to her eyes. Her fingers itched for the familiar weight of a camera, though she knew she'd never be able to capture the feeling in her chest on something as cumbersome as film.

Pushing herself forward on her hands and knees, Abby crawled, the summit barely twenty feet ahead, prairie grass waving at her merrily from the ridge. A laugh bubbled from her throat despite her body's pain and the dryness in her throat. It was a light, bright sound that reminded her of a time long ago. Once, she had run up mountains, and it irked her that she could now barely manage to top what was nothing more than a mound of land.

The blood on her palms had thickened into a paste, gathering a crust of dirt and stones as she used rabbit brush and clumps of grass to pull herself along, battered body screaming for relief. A hawk cried out somewhere in the heavens, but she didn't have the energy to raise her gaze to the sky.

She was almost there.

The stolen truck was abandoned somewhere behind her, out of gas and parked on a narrow track too faint to really be called a road. By her estimation, she'd be long dead by the time anyone managed to find her, but the thought didn't fill her with grief. Too long they'd kept her shut away in the dark, only to let her outside like an ailing pet once or twice a day. She had no family, and there was no one else to mourn her passing. Abby staunchly refused to let death take her while she laid in bed like a frightened child, so she'd made her own arrangements, away from prying eyes and doubting medical doctors. None of them had any idea what she was capable of.

When she finally drug herself the final few feet, the tears that had gathered at the corners of her eyes fell, the moisture coating the once vibrant blue already dulled to gray by age. Gasping with relief, the golden landscape before her beckoned with open arms as she pushed herself up to lean against a large stone.

It was just as she remembered.

The herd of mustangs that grazed in the narrow valley below raised their heads at her arrival, a dun stallion letting out a single snort before returning his watchful gaze to his mares. The horses weren't the same ones she'd photographed years before, but she could still see the resemblance in the painted coats, splashed piano keys of black and white hovering amid the silver brush. Behind the horses, spears of rhyolite grasped at the yellowing sky, bursting from banks of volcanic cinders as the canyon lands and the Owyhee desert widened to touch each horizon. It was blissfully silent, the gentle rustling of the animals as they grazed the only companionship she required.

For the first time in years, Abby felt a peace settle over her.

She'd watched the cities grow, swelling like the cancer eating at her bones, greedily swallowing every inch of land as they replaced gullies with parking lots and prairie grass with subdivisions. Her beloved desert had been pushed further and further away, an ocher ring embracing the monotonous gray and black of humanity's progress.

She'd refused to die in a cesspit.

A contented sigh escaped her as she watched the wild horses, the world gently shifting into the colors of sunset, the bright orb of the sun hovering near the western horizon. Abby knew that she was probably watching her final day on earth fade, but she only hoped that she'd be able to witness the stars spangle before her eyes closed a final time.

Despite the ache in her hands, she dug fingernails into the sun-warmed earth, her heart singing in its unsteady rhythm. The sweat in her hair felt like it belonged there. As she gazed out over the landscape, she couldn't help but feel like she was right where she needed to be. In her mind's eye, the age spots and wrinkles had faded, her hair once again the corn stalk yellow of her favorite buckskin horse. Her legs were strong and steps certain, the world wide and perfect as she watched the desert flourish through the lens of her camera.

Abby smiled at the thought, wishing she could have captured that final image. She had a feeling it would have been perfect.

The horses lingered near long after she let her eyes slip closed, the dusting of clouds in the sky burning crimson as the desert caught the final rays of the fading day. The canyons bowed shadow heads in respect as the wind cried out in mourning against the cliffs.

As the light faded to gray, the desert remained, wide and endless as the mountains guarding the forgotten world of sage and stone. Many had passed through the desolate scrub, always eager to take, to reform and to

judge. The land had waited, enduring, longing for someone who could see—someone who would understand.

Abby's hands never stirred from the dirt. She never
again moved from the chunk of stone where she'd stopped
to rest. But the smile on her face was as clear as the thousand stars that sprang into life in the ebony heavens, her
spirit as free as the desert wind that swayed through the
sage.

IT WAS A DARK AND STORMY NIGHT

Tales from
underneath
the bed.

SUEDEAN MORRIS is a writer, online entrepreneur, co-chair of the Caldwell Writer's Group and proud mother of three. She is happily married and lives in the quirky town of Caldwell, Idaho. When she isn't writing or chasing after a kiddo, she enjoys crafting and adding to her list of things she never thought she would have to say. The most current addition to her list is, "Please don't put your face in the dog's butt."

Imagine
a
killer
using
a
guillotine.

GUILLOTINE

SueDean Morris

T he days blended into each other since that night at the bar. She'd just found out her husband had another wife and three children. Furious and emotionally destroyed with the discovery of the love of her life's treachery, she took off. Two-hundred and fifty miles later she sat at the bar downing shot after shot of whiskey when the mousey-looking man claimed the stool next to her. Not once did his company signal warning, danger, "I will kidnap you". When he asked if she wanted to get a drink in his room, she decided to hell with it. Her husband had built an entire separate life behind her back; why should she be loyal to him?

Hindsight is always a bitch. All the self-defense classes she took in college had the same theme: don't leave a public space with a stranger. The drink he served her in his room was laced with something. She woke up chained and collared like a dog with her hands zip-tied behind her back in a dark metal prison. The mousy bastard hand-fed her like a baby when he decided she needed to eat. His hands would pet her hair or run over her skin in between bites. Each caress had disgust swelling within her.

The screech of the heavy lock being disengaged drew her attention. Mousey Bastard's smile stretched across his face had chills racing down her spine. His overly touchy hands rolled a key back and forth over his palms, taunting her with every rotation. Twisting her wrists in their plastic cuff, she wanted nothing more than to be able to take the key from him. The closer he got the more she felt like she was being stalked. The feeling unnerved her enough to have her attempt to merge with the wall. As his hands made contact with the collar her breath caught. Finally free, she surged toward the freedom that lay beyond the door, barely making it a couple of steps toward her goal when her head was wrenched back, neck arched, as one of his hands grasped her black hair. The second wrapped firmly around her collar. He used his greater strength to march her out of her prison.

In the next room, he propelled her toward a pair of seven foot tall poles, each with its own chain attached at the top. After securing her to her new position, Mousey

Bastard ambled off, whistling a tuneless tune. Time dragged by while she waited for him to return and fear painted images of what her immediate future might look like.

An eternity passed while she waited. Her eyes remained fixed on the door her capturer slinked through. Finally, Mousey Bastard returned leading another man on a leash. By the look of the other man he had been severely beaten. Half his face was an array of purples and yellows, and when he turned so that Mousey Bastard could chain him to the poll on her left, she saw welts and open abrasions zig-zagged his back. Her eyes begged the new guy to do something, anything, to free them both, but he never raised his gaze from the floor.

"Dearly beloved." At the sound of Mousey Bastard's voice, her eyes snapped over to him with dawning horror. Her brain refused to comprehend the situation she was in. After the conclusion of this fucked-up ceremony, in which neither she nor the new guy made a sound, Mousey Bastard released the papers to flutter to the ground. He skipped over to a covered structure and, with a hard pull of the material, revealed a fucking guillotine.

Mousey Bastard stood in front of her as terror-induced tears started trickling down her cheeks. His cold hand cradled her face; his thumb wiped away the tears that continue to fall.

He cooed, "Don't cry. I was able to pick you both up at a bar even though your spouse's ring, his claim on you, was still proudly displayed on your hand." His voice hardened. "There's no space in the world for unfaithful sluts. I bet your other spouses would feel a hell of a lot better knowing in the end you were punished for your infidelity. I know I would have felt better."

He shuffled over to the new guy, her fake husband, unchained and pushed him toward the guillotine. Mousey Bastard arranged the new guy into a position that satisfied him. The new guy ended up on his knees with his neck locked into a stock piece. The demon wearing Mousey Bastard's skin appeared inhuman.

A sick grin twisting his features: Mousey Bastard pulled the lever.

The blade raced down with a "shwick" and new guy's head bounced and rolled a couple times before halting. Blood pumped from his neck, painting the lower half of the guillotine and Mousey Bastard's shoes and pants. He dragged the new guy's headless corpse toward her. Her sobs and pleas and dry-heaving echoed off the walls, building in volume and hysteria with each of Mousey Bastard's progressing steps. Valiantly fighting her collar, she accomplished nothing more than twisting the chain around her head and choking herself.

The demon's fist slammed into her temple, stunning her enough so that she could be unchained. Mousey Bastard manhandled her the same way he brought her into the room. She dug her heels in, jerking, twisting, and wiggling around needlessly while incoherently begging for her life.

Her knees slammed onto the hard floor; strands of her hair knotted in his hand as her head was forced down. The padded cradle of the stock fit her neck like a custom made necklace with a lock for a clasp. Her sobbing escalated. She didn't want to die like this. She didn't want to die at all.

Mousey Bastard's hand gently smoothed and untangled her hair, and with one final stroke he stood. She knew this was her end. The haunting sound of the blade's rushing decent was the final bell of her life.

Not every victim is humanized,
not every killer is caught,
and not every story ends
in happily ever after.

I'M SORRY, BABY GIRL

SueDean Morris

"Elly?" I croak.

Where the fuck is my baby? Where am I? Attempting to look around is exceedingly foolish and yields nothing. My head won't respond. My entire body is completely numb, unwilling to respond to my commands. Panicking, my body twitches, chest tightening, air escaping my lungs but unable to return. The possibility of being drugged peeks through panicking thoughts. My eyes are burning, clenching shut, while tears and snot trickle down the sides of my face, depositing themselves into my hair.

Why? Why me? Where is the man? I think he was at my house. The darkness becomes hazy as my lungs burn before blissful oblivion.

"Please let Elly be alright," I chant over and over still laying prone on the cold, moist ground. My chanting is the only sound penetrating the silence since I woke from my panic-induced slumber. The moon is winking at me through a very small window. The rest of the room is draped in shadows. The moonlight cuts a tiny path through the shadows, revealing stone. I slowly drag myself into a sitting position, while my burning eyes frantically sweep the room for Elly. No Elly. Hopefully this means she is safe with Daddy.

Spotting what I assume is a door, I try to stand, to move over and grab it, but my legs refuse to hold me up. Arms trembling, I'm able to begin to crawl my way toward the door before my arms refuse to hold me up any-more. I sink down, face pressed to the floor, blood and tears mixing, sobs ripping from my chest as I lay there. As soon as the trembling passes, I stretch out my arms and slowly haul myself through inches of dirt and grime covering the floor. Crawling forward bit by bit, slowly moving toward the door, the dirt and grime inch into my white tank top, staining it beyond repair. My arms and bare feet propel me forward, becoming decorated with small cuts and scrapes from the rough surface of the floor against my skin. Finally, as I reach the door, new sobs echo off the walls. It takes multiple tries before I can stabilize myself on my knees. My hand shakes violently as it closes over the door handle. Relief floods my system as prayers spill from my lips that I've made it to freedom.

"No, no, no!" I screech when the handle doesn't budge. Letting the hysterics consume me, I beat on the door until the adrenalin rush depletes itself. What minuscule amount of strength I have drains from my body. Resting the side of my face on the floor, I cry.

Awkwardly, I shuffle myself back into a corner. On my short journey away from the door, I snatch up a rock about the size of my fist. The chilly wall against my back is a small relief. The rock clutched tight in my hands, my eyes grow heavy. My last thought is: I wonder how I got here.

Head throbbing, slowly my eyes peel open, and I beg for my dream to come back. Before waking up in my own personal hell, I was a normal woman with a normal life. Living the American Dream, paying bills, taking care of the home we bought. All I have in this world is a husband and a beautiful daughter. Guilt chokes me as the last conversation between my husband and I plays in my mind: the horrible things I accused him of, the nasty things said. Is he out there looking for me? Or did he think I left him like I said I was going too? He has to know I'm missing. I never picked Elly up from daycare. He has to know I would never abandon our daughter. Right?

All I've ever wanted was happiness. My husband has been working a lot lately, leaving me and the baby alone. I believe his work is more important to him than us. When he's not at work he's either sleeping or playing video games with his friends. My daughter is just like any other little girl her age. She is too curious for her own good and her getting into everything drives me nuts. Trying to find happiness means sacrifices, tears, and pain. In my thirty years, I've had some of the best days of my life: high school graduation, wedding day, and my daughter's birth. I shake my head; I desperately need to find a way out of this prison.

Gloomy, moist, chilly, hard—all of these are perfect ways to describe my cell. The room I'm trapped in is made entirely of grey bricks, walls, floor, and ceiling. In the corner opposite the one I've claimed, a small hole is dug that smells rank. I'm assuming it's a latrine. The cell itself is maybe eight by eight feet. The door is some kind of black metal, embellished with rust spots.

Someone has installed a large mail slot at the bottom of the door. Directly across from the door is a tiny window, situated a little lower than halfway up the wall. Bracing my hands against the wall I stand up and walk over to the window. The top portion of the window rests with my mouth. There are no bars or glass, but it looks too small to fit my frame through. Griping the edge of the hole, I attempt to pull myself up and through. My shoulders refuse to fit. I twist this way and that trying to heave myself through this small hole. Sighing, I give up and walk back over to my corner and slide back down. My eyes lock onto the ceiling, silently counting the abnormally large bricks. I'm terrified.

Has my whole life led up to this moment? Elly, my beautiful baby girl with her chocolate curly hair, hazel eyes full of mischief, an innocent grin spread over her face, and only half as tall as me. I wonder how my baby and my husband are doing. I can't imagine what he's thinking, but he needs to be strong for Elly. Eyes and nose burn as a cascade of tears caress my cheeks. I want to be home, rocking Elly, singing our lullaby. I made it up for her when she had colic and would cry and cry. I paced around our house with her safely cradled within my arms. Leisurely swaying back and forth, eyes trained on the tiny window, cradling the rock, singing softly:

Close your eyes.
Say goodnight.
Go to sleep, Mommy's baby.
I will be here when you wake,
I can promise you that.
Close your eyes, say nah-night.
I will see you when you wake up.

Dragging my hands down my face merely cakes on more grime. I wonder what I'm doing here. My eyes drift over to the wall on my left. I should keep track of how long I've been here.

Heaving myself to my feet, I head over to the hole. As disgusting as shitting in a hole is, I can't hold it in anymore; my bladder and rectum have been warning me for a while now and if I continue to ignore their warnings then I'm going to regret it. Peeling my filthy yoga pants and black underwear down my legs, I squat over the hole. I have no way to wipe. Shit. Reaching back with my right hand I try and get as much fecal matter off my ass as possible.

Righting myself, I reach down to wipe my fingers off on my pants. In a burst of hideous invention, I realize I can keep track of the days using shit as ink, painting one tally mark on the wall for yesterday and another for today. I clean off my fingers to the best of my ability on the bottom of my pants.

The lack of social interaction and silence will soon drive me crazy. I need to find something to think about or something to do. Before being locked into this cell, I spent my days running errands, playing with my baby, reading, crafting. I know I should be spending more time trying to figure out a way home and less time complaining, but I need some form of stimulation. I would love something to do. Great, I am now repeating myself.

The day gradually ticked by while I lay on the chilly bricks, thinking of my friends and family, trying to replay TV shows behind my eyelids, reciting what I can remember from books. The grating sound of metal on metal has my head snapping in the direction of the door. Flipping onto my hands and knees, my shocked eyes lock onto the plastic tray pushed into my cell. I strain my ears, listening for the footsteps. As they fade away, I slowly climb to my feet and go and look at the offering.

The smell is horrible, the water polluted, and the food appears completely inedible, a brown paste. I retch and cough as globs of the paste fall from the spoon, making a squelching noise when they land. Deciding it's for the best if I don't eat, I sip the water cautiously, but refuse to touch any more of the food. When the cup is drained, I place it back by the plate and amble around humming to myself.

As the sun's rays fade I turn my attention to the wall. It's time to add another mark. I use the brown paste this time—the spoon my pen—to add another tally. Tossing the spoon in the direction of the tray, I head over to the sleeping corner, and lay flat on my back with the chill from the bricks seeping through the thin tank top and pants, my right arm under my head, the left stretched out perpendicular to my body. My left hand absently traces the grooves in the brick of my prison. Swallowing a sob, my eyes fall shut and my breathing becomes deep and even.

"I officially hate the sun", my inner voice sings as my eyes flutter open. Standing and relieving myself, I walk over to my window. Outside I see death and sand and a person?

"Hey!" I scream frantically waving one arm through the little window. "Please help me!"

The person transforms into a cactus when I blink.

"Wait! Don't go!"

My words die at the end. The horizon stretches into a distant, grey mountain range, the cactus stands tall and lonely. The rest of the plant life is limp and sunburned, scattered throughout bleak openness. Various cacti scattered around are the only signs of life. I worry that that is a forecast of my future: dead and forgotten. Stumbling back, away from those nasty thoughts, my once clean clothes flutter from the sudden movement—clothes that at one time hugged my curves now hanging off my frame. I know I should be eating when food is offered, but I can only force myself to choke down the pasty shit when the hunger pangs are too much.

Ten tally marks adorn the precious brick. I have been locked in this cell for ten days, maybe more. Day after day, the same. I find ways to entertain myself, stare out into the dead landscape, entertain myself some more, tally the wall, and sleep.

Why does no one ever come in here? Once a day food is pressed through the mail slot at the bottom of the door, and whoever is delivering me food doesn't talk. It's so quiet in here I can hear water trickling down the walls and little creatures playing. It's driving me insane. I bet that's their plan: shatter my mind by complete isolation.

"**It's working,**" I attempt to scream, but it comes out as a croak. I am covered in muck, and smell like I haven't bathed more than ten days. I snicker to myself. I'm so funny sometimes.

Yesterday, at least I think it was yesterday, I spoke with a very kind rat. He told me how to get out of here; I just have to have a body the size of a rat to get through the hole in the wall. I'm not sure how to go about shrinking my body to fit in the tiny hole. Maybe something will come to me later. Thanking the kind fellow, I lunged for him.

I didn't catch the little bastard. He was able to squeeze into the hole and out of my reach. I spent the remaining daylight sitting in front of it, trying to coax him out.

The scraping of the mail slot drew my attention. I watch in fascination as the food is pushed into my room. Getting to my feet, I rush across the room, colliding with the door frame.

"**Hey, what's your name?**" My voice is a whisper, but to my ears it is incredibly loud. The prick or prick-ette said nothing back. How am I supposed to find out what's going on if the only living creature speaking to me is a rat? I'm pretty sure I scared him off.

Sighing, I squat and force down the brown pile of nastiness, and go back to my favorite corner. Before the sun's rays catch me, I use the spoon and mark the wall. Tossing away the spoon and picking up the rock, I watch the sun gradually disappear, the rock safely placed in my lap, slowly running my hand along its smooth surface. Long after darkness creeps into my cell I lie down, curl around it and sleep.

Twenty tally marks glow on the wall. I cover the rest with crude drawings, scribbles. Shit and paste aren't the best tools for drawing. They attract pests, though they are filling.

I'm sure today is going to be a good day. The voice in my head and the sun agree. The door makes a loud clicking noise and I'm stunned when it opens. A hand appears at the door's edge, pushing it wider. The man that enters my room is huge, with yellow hair, cold mud eyes, a hard mouth and jaw, and the rest of him pure muscle.

His appearance shakes me. Weary eyes lock onto him as I slowly scoot myself between the intruder and Elly. He lumbers across the room in my direction, stopping when he towers over my trembling form. His hand strikes out, grabbing a handful of my hair and hauling me to my feet. He turns toward the door and drags me out of the room.

"N-n-no, please!" I cry. "Please! I can't leave, I can't leave Elly again!" I stretch longingly for Elly.

He halts, and his muddy eyes trail over my face, his brow furrowed. "There's no baby in there," he says. "Just a fucking rock."

The brute wraps my hair around one hand while the other tightens like a vice around my upper arm and we're off again. The hallway outside my room is dark. Why is it dark? The brute turns left and sets off at a brisk pace; I don't even try to keep up. I just let myself be dragged like a doll.

A room with a bright red door is our destination. This room is similarly built but at least twice the size of my cell. Whereas my cell was constructed from grey brick, this room has red. In the center of the room with the red brick walls, there's a snow white ceiling, glistening concrete floors indented with four drains surrounding a metal gurney. Right next to the gurney is a metal cart with two shelves. There's nothing on the bottom shelf, but on the top shelf sits a bucket of soapy water, a washcloth, and scissors.

Being lifted like I was nothing is a new experience for me, and the man-mountain was nice enough to set me down gently. I squeal when the cold metal touches my body. He leans over me, his clothing a gentle caress against me as he locks my right wrist into the leather cuff I failed to notice. He straightens up then repeats the same procedure for my left wrist. Moving to where my legs lay limp at the bottom of the table, he locks my legs, one at a time, in the cuffs. I'm now lying on a rapidly warming table completely restrained. The brute, scissors in hands, cuts my filthy clothes off one item at a time. My once pearly white tank top resembles an oil cloth. My comfortable yoga pants are more brown than black. Their new home is the empty bottom shelf of the cart.

I look at him, giggling. **"I'm getting a massage, but shouldn't I be on my stomach for a massage?"** The look he gives me has me reevaluating my sanity. I'm now about a hundred percent sure I'm wrong about the massage.

The voice in my head agrees. The guy leaves the room but doesn't bother shutting the door behind him. Right above the gurney are four metal circles suspended, maybe a few inches, from the ceiling by a chain. I turn my head to the left and look over at the washcloth. It's green, my favorite color. I wonder if the brute knew that.

Hearing footsteps getting louder I turn my head toward the door. The brute walks back in carrying a huge mirror. He attaches it to the circles over the table I am strapped to, and I stare up at my reflection.

Black hair tangled, matted, bloody, soiled, and empty sapphire eyes. The rest of me is filthy and bruised and covered in infected wounds. I wonder where I got the bruises. I gasp when the brute drags the freezing wet green cloth over my face, removing dirt and grime as he went. Time stretches on agonizingly slow as he rubs down my entire body. He exchanges the wash cloth for a pair of scissors. With surprising skill, the brute goes to town gathering chunks of hair and, with a snip and a careless flick of his wrist, discards the freed strands to the floor. His large callused hands shove my head into position for him to continue his work.

Once satisfied, he swaps the scissors for clippers, and repeats the process all over again. After deeming me presentable, he unhurriedly pushes the cart away from me and out the door.

Alone again, I take in the room. The red brick walls fade and become white with green trim; the floor that should have been cement becomes pitch black tile. The table I'm attached to morphs into the softest of beds. Over by the door is my dresser from home, pictures of my family on top. I shake my head. There's no way that's here.

The rhythmic sound of footsteps fills me with anticipation and apprehension. I can't wait to see what's going to happen.

It's the brute again, and behind him a slightly smaller man pushing a cart adorned with some kind of medical equipment, a cloth with multiple wires sticking out in every direction, and a laptop. The man stations the cart behind my head, then goes over to shut and lock the door. I study the smaller man. He has blond hair, icy-blue eyes, a big crooked nose and a straight mouth. The brute is easily a foot taller than the smaller man. Neither speaks a word to me.

The smaller man putters around, setting up. His blue eyes hold no emotion. He stands behind me. The first soft touch of cloth on the sides of my head causes me to jerk forward as far as my binds allow. The smaller man's impatient huff informs me that I shouldn't have moved.

"Chad, hold Number Seven's head still." Chad nods to the smaller man in acknowledgment, and stomps over to my helpless form. His big hands squish the sides of my face together while holding my head completely still. As the cloth blankets my newly shaved head, Chad's hands roughly drag down, pulling my skin with them. Chad continues to hold my head stationary as the smaller man adjusts the cap encasing my skull. With Chad's help, he finishes strapping my head to the gurney.

The rhythmic clicking noise of the smaller man typing away lulls me into drowsiness. Eventually, the silence is interrupted by a conversation between the two. Their words are meaningless, just another background noise. I'm jerked out of my blissful state by a sharp pain in my forehead. That short bastard hit me.

"Number Seven, pay attention." His voice is higher than any other grown man I've heard. Standing on my right side, the smaller man holds a clipboard and a pen. Icy eyes flick between my prone position, the laptop, and his clipboard. His eyes locked firmly on his clipboard, he demands, "Number Seven, do you know where you are?"

All I can do is shake my head. I've always been here.

"Do you know how you came to be here?" he continues.

My eyes closed tightly, my mind racing. The brute at my door—weakly, I point to Chad, hand and voice trembling. **"H-he was a-at my d-d-door."**

The smaller man nods, writing down something on his clipboard. "Yes, and he was at your house. He brought you here for observation. I'm conducting experiments on different physiological weaknesses of humans."

All I could do was nod along dumbly. I knew what some of those words meant separately, but put together they became a foreign language.

"You fit the criteria for social isolation," he continued. "We needed a female in her early thirties. Chad brought me several different women, but I chose you. I wanted to see how long you would last without your baby, though I didn't anticipate you replacing your child with a rock."

The word "baby" sinks into my brain. All at once flashes of a tiny little girl crying, of a baby chanting "mama", of a precious angel trying to run before walking. "B-baby, E-Elly?" pitifully rushes from my mouth. **"S-she's in my r-r-room."**

The scientist looks past me and jerks his head toward the door. Chad stomps past, turns right and disappears, his footsteps getting quieter. The scientist continues to ask me questions: Why did I mark the wall? Why did I sit in a corner? Who was I talking to?

I don't know why I did any of those things. He didn't like my answers.

Chad enters the room carrying Elly. Frantically, I thrash around as much as I can. I beg them to give her to me. I want my baby girl. Chad hands the scientist my Elly.

"**Please!**" Tears and snot poar down my face. "Please don't hurt her! S-She's just a baby!" Hysteria has taken full control of me at this point. I will do anything if they would just let her go.

The scientist turns and throws Elly. My throat tightens as she flies through the air. I watch in shock as she bounces off the ground. Shrill screams erupt, interrupting the stillness of the moment. All I can see is Elly's small broken body laying deathly still on the brick floor, blood pooling around her.

"Number Seven has projected maternal bonds onto a rock." His words bounce around and mix with the sight of Elly around my head. "Her brain activity has given us some great data."

Screams and sobs silence as I lay there staring at Elly. I couldn't protect my baby. What kind of mother was I? She didn't deserve any of this, and I let her down.

I don't react when the restraint holding my head up or the head cover are removed. I tune the two men out. I don't care what happens now. The back of the gurney lowers, laying me flat on my back. Turning my head, I can't take my eyes off Elly.

Movement out of the corner of my eye has me twist my head. There is a strange girl with numb sapphire blue eyes strapped down to a table. We stare at each other. I should know this girl. The nagging feeling I've seen her before takes hold and I want to reach out to this girl and enclose her in my arms where she will be safe. I couldn't protect

Elly, but maybe I could protect her. This protective feeling consumes me.

My eyes linger on the girl in the mirror. The man moves and starts poking around the girl's stomach. His sudden movement makes me glance at him. His eyes have changed from indifference to insane.

The scalpel held aloft over his head, "You helped tremendously with our data, but collecting data isn't the only reason you are here. Death is too good for a worthless mother who would fail her child. You failed Elly." He brought it down repeatedly, puncturing my torso.

There was no girl in the mirror. I had been feeling protective over myself. Screams explode from my mouth as the pain races up and down my nerves. The brute instantly appears at my side with a knife in his hand. I quickly look back up in the mirror at the poor woman who was being tortured. That has to be some other girl. There is no way this is happening to me. I would never have let these sick fucks touch Elly.

Almost as quickly as I start screaming I stop. I watch in silence as the knife presses against her neck just under her jaw and then strokes across her neck. Instantly her neck, jaw, and upper chest is painted red. After a minute of watching her sad face stare back at me, I feel woozy. My eyes refuse to stay open, and my breath leaves me. My final thought is, **"I'm sorry baby girl. Mommy will always love you."**

We all want a body like Adonis.
Sometimes it comes
with strings attached.

GETTING SHREDDED

Andrew Majors

She was short, stocky, with a round face, her torso soft, stomach jutting out slightly from beneath the cardigan she wore. It bobbed gently to and fro as she made her way down the street. The rest of her struck a decent balance: not too much excess in the arms, curves bending outward in the right places on her hips and thighs. Her complexion was milky white. Thick-lensed glasses turned her light brown eyes into high-beams in the afternoon light.

It was likely no one had ever thought of Kathy Haim as beautiful, but beauty, as was often said, lay in the eye of the beholder. To him she was perfect.

He watched until she turned and walked up the drive-way of the large two-story house near the end of the cul-de-sac. When he was absolutely sure she wouldn't see him, he moved. His strides were enormous, chiseled arms and legs swinging, the grey fabric of his straining sweatshirt making them resemble the marble limbs of some enor-mous ghost. The jog to his car a block away took a half-minute. Everything he needed was in the trunk.

It was a quarter to five in late October, six months since the tape.

◄ ❚❚ ►

"Hey Feedbag, free rental."

The edge of the VHS tape caught him in the back of the neck. It didn't hurt, clattering to the floor as Kevin and his friends burst out laughing.

That hurt, but he'd expected it—like he'd been expect-ing it ever since second grade, when he realized he was the only kid his age with a gut, that he ran slower than every-one else, that he couldn't do pushups or sit ups without getting sick, and that the other kids thought pointing the-se things out over and over again was the peak of hilarity.

Resisting the urge to whip the tape back at Kevin, he bent over and picked it up. From the cover he could tell what shelf it had come from. A blond man stood on a white beach, arms akimbo, naked apart from a Speedo pat-terned with the world's least respectable American flag. His grin was as ebullient as Florida sunshine. Sunglasses both made him super cool and replaced his eyes with shin-

ing coal pits. Every square inch of him, from neck to calves, was an undulating bronze prairie of perfectly toned muscle.

The label read: FAT TO ALL THAT! GET A BEACH BOD IN ONLY 90 DAYS!

"Ninety years wouldn't help you, Feedbag," Kevin's friend Kyle snickered, knocking into him as he made his way to the counter. Kevin's other friend Jacob tried slapping his stomach as he passed by but added nothing further. Tape still in hand, he made his way to the counter to ring them up, and then they were gone. It was three o'clock. Rewind Rentals stayed open till six.

He straightened shelves, dusted, served the few other customers that came in over the next two hours. It was a decent job that paid well enough, and Mr. Hartley even trusted him enough to let him lock up on weeknights, a sight more than what most other adults gave him, which was either pity (which they suspected he wanted) or silent contempt (which they figured he deserved).

He didn't try to be overweight. He exercised, ate right, but his exercise was always half-assed and his willpower was never enough, so he was and would likely always remain "Feedbag".

Workout tapes belonged on the shelf near the door. He walked over and placed the copy of FAT TO ALL THAT! back in its proper place. Then he noticed the blank tape, the kind that usually had another one with a real cover in front of it, sitting there like an empty canvas. Without thinking, he grabbed it.

There was nothing on the front or back—no beaches, no parading specimens of human perfection, male or otherwise—just a sheet of blank white copy paper with a title typed on it in tiny, barely legible letters: GET SHREDDED. The rest of the tapes had colorful labels, glossy pictures, wonderful promises, but this one just had a command.

Get shredded.

He didn't know why he took it with him at the end of his shift. Later on, he liked to think it had chosen him, like it had so many before. He figured he had nothing to lose, that maybe even a feedbag like him could somehow "get shredded".

He was right.

◀ ❚❚ ▶

Kathy first saw him after the Kellerman twins were in bed and she was downstairs, doing her usual halfhearted cleanup in an attempt to leave the places she sat for a bit neater than she'd found them. He was tall, his torso a slab of meat ballooning out above the waist, his legs sticking out beneath it like tree trunks. His clothes looked at least three sizes too small. There was bare skin where the seams of his jeans had popped. His face was shadowed under the blinding halo of the streetlamp, but she could see something in his hand—a long, thin object that glinted.

She saw him for an instant, nothing more. Twenty minutes later, when cleanup was done and she was on the couch taking advantage of the Kellerman's cable hookup, he was still watching her.

◄ ❚❚ ►

He watched the tape that night in the basement where Dad kept the spare TV. He was at work, and Mom was at her book club. At first it looked broken. Then the static lines cleared and he saw a grey-haired man in a suit jacket standing in front of an off-white background. He watched, clad in shorts and a t-shirt, as the man began to speak in a clear, concise voice with a stern, almost machine-like tone:

"Welcome to 'Get Shredded', the all-body bodybuilding video gateway to a better you. For beauty and health reasons as well as reasons of the mind, it is imperative you follow closely along with the provided program. All steps herein are part of getting shredded, and should be repeated as necessary. The program will never deviate. You must never deviate. The program will cease only once you are shredded. If you are not totally shredded you must continue. Please watch, work out, and enjoy. And remember: quitters never win."

The man disappeared, replaced by an ant race that went on for a few more minutes. He limbered up as best he could, bending listlessly from side to side and attempting in vain to touch his toes. Then the regimen started.

The first shot showed a man and woman in workout clothes. The woman was a frizzy-haired angel in form-fitting spandex, doing step-ups on a small platform. The man wore nothing but workout trunks, the old Fifties kind, performing reps on a bench beside her with a set of hand weights. Both stared straight ahead, not at the camera but off into the distance somewhere. In the background he heard easy listening music filtered through a shitty set of speakers.

"Get shredded," the man said with each rep.

"You want this," the woman said.

Cut to another scene. The man and woman were now both on the bench, the man on top of the woman, his hands around her throat. Both of them still looked like they had been lobotomized.

"You want this," he said as her head lolled back, mouth wide open. "Get shredded."

Another cut. Blood. The woman gurgled. The man gnashed his teeth.

"Eat clean."

Another scene, and another, and another. He saw dozens of people doing everything to each other. The off-white walls spattered red. They all got a good workout in, saying:

"Get shredded."

"Get ripped."

"Train hard."

"Don't lie."

"Inhale, exhale."

"Be the wolf, be the lion."

"Break free."

"Ten more reps."

"You want this."

"Get shredded."
He watched the whole thing. All four hours.

◄ ❚❚ ►

The knock at the door sounded like someone fired a cannon, and if not for a glance out the bay window to the right she would have opened it right away. What she saw froze her dead to the ground.

The man from across the street was now standing at the door, what passed for his face still invisible to her. His body which had seemed so solid was nothing but an amorphous mass. His sweats, rent open at the chest, revealed acres of bulbous, throbbing flesh. Whatever he had been holding was now buried in the folds of a gelatinous arm barely reined in by a tattered sleeve.

He knocked again, louder. The doorframe began to splinter.

◄ ❚❚ ►

His gut no longer spilled over the top of his boxers, and his arms and legs, though still just tubes of meat, were shaping up, displaying the promise of tone. The same had occurred with his legs, calf and thigh muscles, all of them now bulging in ropelike cords. His face was unrecognizable, like it had been sculpted by powerful invisible hands into having a chin and cheekbones for the first time. No flab, no stretch marks. He could bend over, run faster, jump higher, and breathe easier, as if his lungs and muscles had been scraped clean. His acne had even started clearing.

Tonight would be watch number seven. He would watch until he had the regimen memorized, then return the tape to Rewind Rentals. Mr. Hartley wouldn't even know it was missing.

Just a few more weeks, maybe even a couple days.

He showered, changed clothes, left for school. The tape stayed beneath his bed.

Next to his workout tools.

◄ ❚❚ ►

The call came at 9:47 and lasted forty-five seconds. The woman on the other end was calm, but her voice began shaking when wood started to crack and something like a burlap sack slammed onto the floor. She rapidly became alarmed, then hysterical. She began screaming. Something was coming in through the door and it had a knife—

The phone fell from her hand, but unspeakable sounds carried through.

◄ ❚❚ ►

The first was George Palmer, age fifty-seven, manager of a Piggly Wiggly over in Germantown. He was fat. He'd been fat his whole life and had never bothered being anything else, figuring death would come for him soon enough whether he looked like Jackie Gleason or Jack LaLanne. He was right.

They found him on the afternoon of June twelfth, remains propped against the store's rear delivery door, his throat torn out, his left arm gone. The rest of him had spoiled in the heat. The cut was clean, surgical, as if guided by master instruction or skill. Police were baffled, his widow devastated.

The next was Phil Kemp, sixty-one, a dentist over in Fayetteville. He was big too but looking to get back in shape for a charity marathon. They found him in the park after Independence Day. He'd crawled into a bike tunnel, his left leg and part of his right foot missing. Again the same precision. An animal had done a bit of gnawing at his throat.

The two cases remained unconnected until early August, when they found Andrea Bell, seventy-nine, a widower in Smith's Corner who'd lost her husband to a stroke. She died at home in the comfort of her favorite chair. Someone had opened her prodigious chest and absconded with her heart, but not before gouging the same bloody smile into the turkey flesh of her neck.

Victor Trask, fifty-three, Rutledge, obese—both lungs.

Charles Andretti, forty-seven, Weston, slightly overweight—assorted entrails.

Fanny Larson, thirty-one, Markland, just a bit hefty—one kidney and part of her liver.

By summer's end there were ten known victims, at least five others suspected, and no leads.

He was very careful, never sharing the regimen with anyone, never working out where he usually went. Some nights he went miles out of his way to towns he'd never been to in his life. The only pattern was his method, the calling card of the mystery suspect the kids referred to as the "Fatty Slasher" and the "Sumo Strangler". He let the regimen guide him and his body do the heavy lifting. As long as he did that he knew, somehow, they would never catch him.

His body became a temple to his devotion. His arms and legs were great pistons that shot out like cobras, his torso a glacier of solid muscle. By now there was no flab anywhere. He felt like he could do anything, like he was invincible.

He kept the bits he took, savoring them, cooking them out in the woods or well off the side of the highway on the way home. He was eating well.

◄ ❚❚ ►

The most disturbing case he'd ever worked—closed.

Detective Hawley sat at his desk. They'd gotten there in the nick of time, just after the bastard had knocked the door off its hinges and stormed inside but before his latest target suffered the sting of a butcher's knife. The perp had been a monster of a man, a roaring four hundred pound mass of stinking meat that could barely stand on two legs. It had taken the boys twenty-eight shots. The girl was in the hospital, still in shock. He'd almost bitten her throat open before tearing away her sweater to try and cut out her stomach.

No ID yet, but the body was barely cold on the slab, and the autopsy was finished. Maybe something in it could tell him why the kid had gone off the deep end. He doubted it, but a man could dream.

He opened the file. As he read, bitter anticipation turned to shock.

The kid had almost no fat beneath his skin.

No fat. Just pure muscle.

◄ ‖ ►

The big dude on the screen spoke like a robot, dressed in a crappy sport jacket and sweatpants ensemble that barely girdled his waist—a total feedbag who could stand to lose a few himself. Not the best spokesman. He stood there impatiently listening to the spiel:

"Welcome to 'Get Shredded', the all-body bodybuilding video gateway to a better you. For beauty and health reasons as well as reasons of the mind, it is imperative you follow closely along with the provided program."

The tape came from the evidence locker. He'd lifted it during his shift. One watch would do it. One watch and he would be in fighting shape. Then he could finally get out of the fucking desk job and back in the field.

What could he say? He wanted a regimen that was right for him.

"And remember," the man said, his hollow little eyes staring off into a far corner of oblivion, "you can do it."

Damn right, fatty, he thought, and as the scenes played he tasted the blood in his mouth, saw his hands around their necks, felt himself getting shredded.

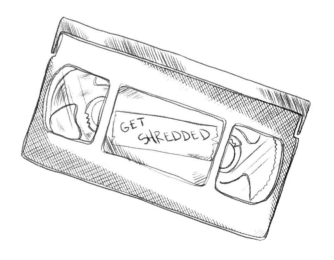

MERRI HALMA has been writing since she was eleven or twelve. Writing provided her with a voice she did not have due to a speech impediment. It was also a way for her to channel her active imagination. She lives in Nampa, Idaho, with her husband, son and two hungry cats.

Mrs. Halma is the author of the Indigo Travelers Series, which includes four books so far, and Haunting of Powell Hall, a paranormal/romance. Her books can be found on Amazon.

What would you do
if you got sent to live with your
aging grandma and find
a mysterious chest?
Would you open it?
What could go wrong?

THE MYSTERIOUS CHEST

Merri Halma

I approach my grandma's house with sweaty palms, gripping my suitcase with all the clothes I own inside. It is my chance to start anew. According to my mom, I needed a firm hand to raise me. But this old house, graying planked wood, three-storied with a wrap-around porch popular in the early 1930's, and double doors had haunted my nightmares. It was supposed to be three stories, but there was an eagle's nest type attic.

I was six the last time I visited. I remembered it smelled musty and ancient then. I see someone, dressed in a penguin suit, peering out behind a curtain, but he vanishes while I am still observing him. He looked ancient, probably had been here since the house was built. Why would this person wear a tuxedo in the middle of the afternoon? Especially in the 21st Century.

My heart is thumping a warrior beat. I had to be strong. I could not let my mom win this battle. She exiled me for taking debating class: that meant I was automatically in the debate club, too. I was also awarded the lead role in my old school's fall production of *Lizzy Borden, Ax Murderer.* Both classes and activities went against my mom's rules and teachings: young women did not learn to speak their minds or argue with men, young women did not seek attention, and young women must adhere by their parents' rules and instructions.

I refuse to bow down to authority. I am who I am. I looked to my dad for support. He just shrugged his shoulders. "Whatever your mom says is good for me, honey. You know she doesn't practice what she preaches."

I want to turn around and flee this house. I remember the strange whispers late at night and eerie eyes watching me, waking me up in the middle of the night, glowing eyes watching every move I made. The memory sent chills and up and down my spine. My parents had chalked it up to my childish active imagination to explain away my fears. I start up the walk, glancing up at the eagle's nest. It is still empty. Grandma lived alone. I'm not sure what I saw. If she took in a lodger, then I am sure I will meet him sooner or later.

As I climb the steps to the house, I feel eyes drilling a hole in my back, causing the hair on the back of my neck to stand at attention. In response, all my muscles tense as I straighten my slumped shoulders. I reach the flat sidewalk and turn around. The street is empty. A light breeze blows a few tumbleweeds and an empty pop can down the road. I see a 2020 Kia Soul parked in the driveway of one of the neighbors. The emptiness fills my being, squeezing my soul. I didn't remember this area being so quiet. Especially with it being so close to four o'clock on a Friday. *School buses should be coming to deposit kids at their homes,* I think. *Or playing outside if they are already home. Deep breaths*, I tell myself as I inhale to steel my nerves, and slowly exhale to try to relax. *I'm going to be okay. I will get through this.*

The front doors are made of firm wood with a glass embossed image of flowers and butterflies on one side and a dragon guarding its hoard of jewels and gold on the other. The dragon turns to me and spits a ball of fire, causing me to jump back and close my eyes to shield them. Slowly, I open them to find the dragon is still part of the glass and gazing at the other side as if it never moved. More chills rush through my veins.

"I must be seeing things, thanks to my active imagination," I mumble under my breath. Still, I feel a thousand eyes watching me. I hear a few whispers and muffled laughter. I turn slowly around, sure I would find mischievous children. No one is there. I curl my hand into a fist to knock.

Before I do, the front door opens with a squeaky of old wood that is seldom used, and I am bombarded with the scent of musty old people. The house needs to be aired and thoroughly cleaned.

"Hello? Grandma?" I say, tiptoeing in. I glance around the corner of the door. No one is there. I hear the TV in the sitting room. I step further in, and the door closes behind me. I walk towards the right of the hallway, where the sitting room is. Grandma is sitting on an old-fashioned flower sofa from the 1940s. She inherited it from her parents. A game show plays on a box TV with legs, and rabbit ears, though there was a modern Satellite box on top of the TV. I am sure that it probably still had tubes inside. *No one would be able to replace those*, I thought, *if one burned out.*

"Oh, hello, dear. I didn't hear you come in," Grandma greets me, putting aside the afghan she is knitting. "I didn't know it was Friday already. I seldom get visitors." She stands, comes over to me and gives me a hug. She is wearing an old pair of jeans with an elastic waistband and a tan sweater.

"Come in, come in. I will show you to your old room. It has been so long since I've seen you. What are you now, thirteen?"

I giggle, but inside I want to scream. I did my best to hide my unhappiness. "No, Grandma. I'm sixteen. I'm old enough to drive, but mom doesn't want me driving. She says buses are safer. She and dad drive all the time. Why can't I learn?"

Grandma smiles condescendingly and pats my arm. "There, there. Be patient with your mom. She is doing what she thinks is best."

"By ruining my life? All I want is to make my own decisions!" I snap. Inside I visualize a lion roaring or a wild bull snorting and pawing the ground; I wished I hadn't bit my grandma's head off. I lowered my head and breathed out my frustration. "I'm sorry. I shouldn't be taking my frustration out on you."

"It's okay, dearie. I will show you to your room and you can tell me all about this injustice you feel. I hear you disobeyed your mom. What was it you did?"

I sigh, shaking my head, not wanting to admit it as we climb the steep steps up to the second floor. "I registered for debate class which automatically put me on the debate team and tried out for the school play, *Lizzie Borden, Axe Murderer.* I won the role of Lizzie. I expected mom to be pleased with me. Instead, she yelled at me for disobeying her. She withdrew me from school and sent me here. She expects you to teach me to respect her. I'm supposed to be a submissive young woman and not speak my mind or argue." I growl, gritting my teeth. Grandma chuckles again.

"Your mom was a lot like you when she was young. At age nine, she was burning her bra and running away to protest against the Vietnam War. You know, there were young kids in elementary, high, and junior high school protesting the war in those days. It wasn't just the college students. She wanted to be a hippy at a young age," Grandma laughed.

"Burning her bra at age 9? Was she even wearing a bra that young?" I knew some girls start wearing a training bra around age 8 or 9, so maybe it was true.

I am amazed, trying to imagine my mom as a free loving hippy. I suck my lips in consideration. That didn't seem quite right. I remember mom saying Grandma spoke of that time. I wonder if it wasn't Grandma that was the free loving hippy. "Wasn't mom born in 1987?"

Grandma nods. "Yeah, yeah. You might be right about that. I can't really remember anymore. I suppose that was me. I wasn't one to obey my parents and I taught your mom to stand up for herself. I guess now she wishes she wasn't so forward and assertive." Grandma turned right. The room was exactly like I remembered it.

Except, there was a large wooden chest at the foot of the bed.

"This is the room you always used, Taylor. Do you remember it?"

I look around, nodding that I did. It had same portraits by two master painters, William Gainsborough's *Blue Boy* and Van Gogh's *The Starry Night*, and one of wild horses running on an open range. I always imagined the horses beckoning to me to run wild with them. It comforted me to see it, reminding me it is okay to be wild and run free. But the chest was odd.

"Yes, I remember it, Grandma. Except for this chest. I don't remember it. Where did you get it?"

"Oh, that old thing? I had it in the attic. Mr. Burton brought it down for me ages ago. Never open it. Never ever open it."

I pat it. "Why?" I ask, hearing something inside pat the lid back. I freeze.

The lights blink off for about ten seconds. Grandma mutters something about poor wiring that old Mr. Burton was supposed have fixed, but never did. When they come back on, the room is arranged slightly differently, with curtains of dainty flowers on them. The bed is now a prin-cess type with a mirror over the bureau and Grandma's clothes changed to an old dress from the early 1950s or 1960s. *Maybe I imagined her dressed some other way, I think.* I blink- *this must be a nightmare.*

Grandma smiles in an eerie way and says, "You re-member the story of Pandora's Box?" I nod. "If that chest is ever opened, it will let out worse creatures than she let escape. And there will be no hope at the bottom."

I suck in my lips, considering Grandma's words. "But we always have hope. Like, I hope the school here has a debate club and team and that it isn't too late to join it." I try to hide my nerves which are sending me several signals that I should not have says that out loud.

Grandma chuckles again. "I wouldn't worry about that. Your mom sent me a list of the acceptable classes for a young woman."

I grimace. *She sent a list?* "She would do that just to ruin my life!"

Grandma says, "First of all, we throw out her list and allow you do what you think is best."

A wave of relief washes through me at that, even though I know mom would not be pleased.

Grandma continued, "Second, you need new jeans."

I look down at my favorite jeans I own - they came pre-ripped. I love the holes because they showcase my tan legs in just the right spots. I worked hard on this tan. I wore them with the best tunic I could find, too, that ended right below the right hip and is a little longer at the left one. The collar fell exactly right over my left shoulder. My left side is my best side. As an aspiring actor for stage and screen, I had to know which side of my body to show to the camera or stage audience.

"Why? These are my favorite jeans. And if you allow me to take the classes I want, then it would be okay for me to dress how I want, too."

"They're already torn, dear. You need new jeans with no rips or tears."

"But, Grandma, all jeans come pre-torn now. It is the latest fashion. If I wear non ripped jeans, I will become an outcast!" I respond, pouting.

"Honey, you already are an outcast! In my day, fashion didn't spread to all areas of the country at the same time. Here, in Stillwaters, we adhere to the old ways. Young ladies must wear acceptable clothes that cover their legs. We don't want the men to notice we have them. Our lower bodies must be a mystery to be unwrapped after matrimony."

Her words hit me like a slap to the face which slid down my esophagus, landing like a ten-thousand-pound boulder in the pit of my gullet. I grimace.

With that, Grandma leaves the room. I turn to my suitcase, reflecting on what my grandma says about my clothes as I unpack. She did wear old clothes, sack dresses that went down to her ankles with dainty flowers on them. I couldn't imagine she ever burned her bra as she claimed, because I never noticed her wearing a bra at all. Then I paused to correct myself. She wasn't wearing those types of clothes, was she? I sigh. I feel confused and perplexed;

being here is strange, something like a nightmare. The lights blink off and on again.

Stillwaters. I don't remember the town being named that. It used to be Kellogg. When did it change its name? Or did I just step into an episode of *The Twilight Zone?* I I hear Rod Serling's deep voice introduce the episode:

Taylor Manchester came from a prestigious family with a bright future ahead of her until one misstep her exiles from her family and she is sent to the forgotten town of Stillwaters, Idaho. Unbeknownst to her, she has just stepped into another dimension.

I giggle to myself, glancing around for hidden cameras. I know I won't find any, but still. Grandma's footsteps fade in the background. I can hear her pleasantly humming and opening cabinet doors downstairs. The lights in the room blink on and off. The silence grows. I hear the revving of a car engine. I go to the window to look out.

One lone car, a 1950 Studebaker, went by. I also notice the car parked in the driveway is now an Edsel. I shiver. I hear *Twilight Zone* introduction music playing in the background.

A knock interrupts the silence. I turn around to see no one standing at the door. The knock comes again. I realize it is coming from the chest.

I walk to the chest and bend over it to whisper, "Hello?"

"Let me out," says a muffled voice.

"Who are you?"

"Your worst nightmare. Or maybe your best friend that will become your worst nightmare."

"No! Grandma told me not to open the chest."

"All is well as long as it doesn't end well. I see your heart. Taylor Manchester, you don't belong here."

"I know I don't. But I have no home. My mom kicked me out for not obeying her."

"Disobeying is your greatest talent. Think, who opened the front door to let you in this house?"

"No one. It opened by itself." I reply. I remembered the eerie feeling when the door opened by itself. Maybe I should have asked.

"Think, Taylor. Hasn't your grandma changed her attire without going to her bedroom?"

I jerked upright quickly, realizing when I first came in, Grandma was wearing old jeans with an elastic waistband and tan sweater with a bra. Now she is in an old a dress with a floral pattern from the 1940s or 1950s. Her breasts sagged, too, because she wasn't wearing a bra. Now, a moment ago, her clothes did change. I heard the melody of *Twilight* Zone play as a shiver travels through my central nervous system.

It bugs me. *Who did open the front door?* Leaving my unpacking 'til later, I dash out of the room and head downstairs to find out. I found her in the kitchen putting water on to make tea and hot chocolate. She had cut fresh tomatoes and had placed them on a plate that also had sliced cheese and crackers.

"Grandma, who opened the front door to let me? You said you didn't hear me knock. I didn't knock because it just opened before I could."

She turns to me. "Why, Burton. He always answers the door."

"Burton? But I didn't see him."

"Of course not, Taylor. Burton doesn't like to reveal himself anymore. You remember Burton, don't you? He used to help me in the gardens and with the landscaping. He died about fifteen years ago, but never left. He enjoys welcoming guests. You were always his favorite because you spoke your mind."

Burton. Mr. Burton. No I don't remember him. I can't place him at all. Hmm.

"Grandma, I don't remember Mr. Burton," I reply thinking, trying to remember. Somewhere deep in my past, I remembered mom mentioning a Mr. Burton. He helped raise her and her siblings. Mom says Mr. Burton had been with grandma since she was a girl. Knitting my brow in confusion, I decide to try this, though know I might be shot down.

"Wasn't Mr. Burton the butler in your childhood home? And after you grew up, you kept him in your house because he didn't have a family?"

The tea kettle whistled. Grandma crossed the room, picked it up, turned towards me with a dark expression on her face, then smiles as she turns back to the teapot and pours the boiling water over the bags. Picking up the tray of snacks with the teacups and tea pot on it, she carries it to the table. I follow, not sure what is going through her mind.

"It was a long time ago, Deary. Mr. Burton was a warlock." She pauses and looks at me. Her strange hazel eyes twinkle, reflecting the chandeliers over the dining room table. "He died so long ago." Then they turn cold as the lights fail, yet again. This time they stay off about ten minutes. Lightning flashes, spotlighting a skeleton wearing Grandma's dress, which is now a floral sack type from the early 1900s, standing near the table holding the tea tray, flapping its flimsy jaw about the faulty wiring that Mr. Burton was supposed have fixed two months ago. The flash ends. Thunder shakes the whole building at the same time as a loud crash of the tea tray, the pot and cups shattered as they land on the bare wood floor adjacent to me. It echoes through the bottom floor, both jarring me so bad, I think my heart stopped. When the lights come back on, Grandma is gone. All that is left is a pile of bones and the floral dress. I stare at them and the broken chinaware and spoiled snacks.

"Taylor," the voice calls from inside the mysterious chest. "It's time to let me out."

With trembling limbs, I walk up the stairs, wondering what just happened. "Grandma, where are you are?" I call, not wanting to believe she just melted like that.

"No one is here but me! Come and see. Will I be an angel? Or will you find the demon of your worst nightmares?"

"I don't want to know," I answer truthfully. The words of a song by a black metal group come to mind, about a person just beginning to explore the darkness only to find himself following the light. I have always strived to follow the light. Now I found myself plunging into deepest darkness of despair.

I turn on the hallway light once I make it to the second floor and go into my room. The chest has moved from its place at the foot of the bed but was still by the bed. It sit between the corner of the bedpost and the chest of drawers.

"Taylor, I smell your cologne. You always wear the sweetest fruit nectar. Open the trunk so I can taste the juice of its essence."

I pause. I don't wear cologne. I paint my nails and style my hair, but I refuse scents because it bothers my sinuses. I don't wear make-up for the same reason. The chest rattles more. It begins to rock back and forth from corner to corner to in its effort to walk towards me. My eyes bug out.

"I see you, Taylor. Wherever you go, I will follow you until you open this chest. When you were young, you dreamed about being a pirate hunting for buried treasure. I could be full of all the jewels you ever dreamed of. Now, here I sit. Right before you."

"No! I never wanted a chest that talked to me! I never wanted forsaken jewels. I wanted books and adventures. Who are you? What do you want with me?"

"Open this chest. You will see."

I run out the door and the chest clumsily follows me, thumping and bumping. The lights blink again. I run down the stairs, looking for something to break the demon chest apart in hopes of killing it. An axe with blood stains appears in my hands. I turn back towards the stairs determined to break it apart. I run towards the stairs.   Before I reach them, the mysterious chest comes tumbling down the ten flights stairs. It land on its lid at the bottom. I think it may have killed itself. Then it starts rocking back and forth with an effort to get up. Whatever is trapped inside laughs manically. Cautiously, I approach it, and find a key taped to the back of it. I unlock the wooden chest.

Out pops a man in a butler uniform. He had to be the one I saw in the window earlier. Only he is a skeleton. He laughs, stepping out, and as he does his skin grows back. "Where is she?"

"Where is who?" I ask, stuttering. "You're Mr. Burton, aren't you?"

"Yes! She killed me and locked me in the chest when I refused to hide anymore of her victims. Where is she? I have haunted this place while I waited for my time. Still opening doors for those that came. For fifty years, I've stayed, trapped in there, watching, waiting and planning my sweet revenge!"

"Grandma's gone! She disappeared. What do you want with me?"

"To eat you instead. To take my revenge on you and all your relations for making me serve you all for years without a care or concern! I'm just a lowly butler! I am much more than that! I'm a human being!"

"I don't remember you. You know all about me."

Burton steps out of the chest, his foot, not yet re-formed, falls from the body. He pulls his other foot out, and it falls off, too. All he has are his ankle bones, and he begins chasing me, demanding the axe. I run upstairs: he follows, the clicking of his bare ankle bones resounding through the house. In the background the wind continues to roar, thunder crashes and the rain pounds the old house.

The closet doors open and more skeletons pour out, joining the chase.

"How do I battle these skeletons? And where did they all come from?" I yell.

"We are your grandma's murder victims. She killed us with that axe you hold. You are no better than her if you use it on us," they taunt. "This is Lizzie Borden's house. You are just like your grandma. You wield the axe she killed us with."

I shiver. This can't be real! This must be a nightmare. I try to wake up.

Turning I run towards them, remembering I used to be a star track sprinter back in the day. I catch one and chop it up, as it laughs, taunting me. Blood from the skeleton splashes all around me, getting all over my prize holy jeans. Blood and bone fragments cover my face, nails, and splatter the walls. Screams erupt from their jaws, echoing through the house.

Soon, I am on my last murder victim, laughing at the joy and freedom I feel. Bodies, not skeletons, lay in front of me when a piercing foghorn erupts the moment. I hear the front door open downstairs as someone calls up.

"Taylor, it's time to wake up. You're miss the bus."

I turn over, slapping the snooze on my phone's alarm.

"Just a few more minutes, Mom."

I lay there, thinking about the dream. After all, Lizzie is a shirttail relative. I toss the covers off. Maybe mom is right about me not being in the lead role. But I will stay in debate class and on the team.

They are many tales floating around
that describe what Hell looks like,
but none are as
terrifying as this.

A Party in Hell

SueDean Morris

I've been wandering through this labyrinth for ages. The same ashy rock structures, the same dry heat. Every path is the same as the last. Fuck, even the torches placed high upon the cavern walls are the same.

My ears perk up as the screams of children echo in the distance. I twist left on the ball of my foot, rushing down another passageway. The screams steadily get louder the further I go. I'm honestly not sure why I'm running toward the children. I didn't like children, so I never brought any of the little parasites into the world myself. When did the ashy toned rock turn dark red? Where the fuck am I?

The last thing I can remember was driving down the interstate to my special play area, with my latest victim passed out in the backseat. He was an imbecile that thought with his stupid pickup line I would mount him, and become some other nameless slut he could brag about to his friends later. Men like him disgust me. They think that because they were physically attractive, women should be grateful for the attention these lowlifes bestow on them.

When I first went to college, my naiveté blinded me to a stupid son-of-a-bitch that acted this way. At first he was so sweet. His blue eyes would focus only on me and it made me feel so special. His strong arms would wrap around my wait making me feel safe. After two weeks of dating, I wouldn't have sex with him so he beat the shit out of me.

Waking from that beating, it felt like the light came on in my head, and I realized what my path in life would be. Bashing his face in with a hammer cemented that path. I felt whole for the first time in my life. The sight of his broken face, blood, and pieces of bone and brain matter splattered around was exhilarating. It was euphoric.

The sudden silence forces my attention back to the situation at hand. Standing directly in front of me is one of those beautiful men that I hate. His blond hair is spiked up, blue eyes narrowed, and that stupid smirk on his face practically begs me to rip his eyes out. "Who the hell are you?" I spit.

His smirk widens and his smooth voice caresses the silence. "I'm Lucifer. Girl, do you know what this place is?"

Now I'm pissed. "Does it look like I know what this hellhole is supposed to be?" My tone is sharp.

"What a very good girl." Lucifer's hand is smoothing my brown hair back away from my face. His skin is silky smooth as it brushes over my forehead.

Lucifer's voice hardens. "You're in Hell for being a very naughty little girl. Did you really think that there would be no consequences for your new hobby? That if the mortal police never caught you, you would've made it into Heaven even though you really enjoyed your little killing spree?"

The smirk that spans his face melts into a neutral mask. My heart is attempting to beat through my ribs.

"You violently abused and tortured twenty different men. Unfortunately for you, your car blew a tire, causing it to collide into a tree." Lucifer tone is cheerful. "I believe the mortals constantly preach using a seat belt, but you thought yourself invincible. You were wrong."

His hand tightens in a punishing grip on my hair, pulling, causing my neck to arch. His rigid grip could rip my hair out by the roots if he chose. He leans down until his face is two inches from mine, whispering, "Now you get to spend eternity here, with the other degenerates. Get up and go help the others with the festivities. I will be around to check on you."

I lay there on the ground, legs stretched out, arms limp at my sides, and my head in the same position Lucifer left me in. The screeching roared to life again. Fear of the penalty of not doing what I was told unfreezes my body. Slowly climbing to my feet, I stumble through a dark red brick arch.

The sight of the absolute chaos has my knees locked and my body refusing to move any further into the abyss. The other adults, attired in turquoise blue V-neck shirts, khaki pants, and white tennis shoes with little party hats of varying color perched atop their heads, shuffle around. Glancing down I'm shocked to see the same outfit draped over my body. Forcing myself to look up, I see a room with parallel rows and columns of picnic tables placed about six feet apart that goes on as far as my eyes can see. The tables are enveloped by vomit-colored tablecloths bathed in cakes, kid drinks, and presents. A "Happy Birthday" sign floats over each table, and balloons in all colors imaginable float around. The adults shuffle around trying to round up all the children—except the children are nothing more than shadows crowned with colorful birthday hats running amok.

The screams, laughter, and fighting of miniature shadows dominate the room. They dart around playing balloon volleyball while the adults, prisoners, are trying to corral them into the next event for the party. Inching forward I reach the first table where ten of the shadows rest along the bench seat on both sides. These little demons vibrate with energy. Upon reaching the table, all ten shadow children leap to their feet and scatter.

What the fuck! Frantically, as I look around for the shadow children of this table my eyes land on another adult that is slowly making her way in my direction. This woman's body is haggard. Her hunched shoulders and limp and greasy waist length black hair accent the pitiful creature heading my way. A green party hat is perched mockingly atop her head. This poor creature's clothes and hair are decorated with juice and cake stains. Her sunken, downcast eyes stare at the floor.

"You are supposed to pour juice, cut the cake, and have the birthday child open presents while all the other children are sitting at the table." She informs me, her defeated voice barely audible over the sounds of the little fiends.

Looking around I try to find the little shadows I'm supposed to round up. I can't distinguish one of the little parasites from the others. Shaking my head I ask this defeated creature, "How am I supposed to accomplish that?"

Her shoulders slump even further. "That is for you to figure out. Just know that if he comes in and you are just standing around, the punishment is horrendous." With that she turns and shuffles off to her own table. That tells me absolutely nothing. How do I get these demons back to the table?

Joining a group of other adults, I call out attempting to be heard over the horde of the tiny shadows. Over and over I holler out: "Hey kids it's time for cake and presents! Who wants some juice? Come sit at the table so we can get the party going!" The other prisoners call out similar incentives. Time is nonexistent in this endless room. It feels like I've been trying to wrangle shadows for eternity, slowly moving around the room calling out and begging the shadows to come to order. I've accomplished nothing. I'm sure I'm not even being heard over the intertwining sounds from the little shadows and the desperate adults being amplified by the room. The sounds reverberating are defining. My hands shake as they cover my ears, trying to block out some of the sounds.

I survey the area hoping that I will spot one of the shadow children that is supposed to be sitting at my table. Angled into the corner of the room is a rundown stand with a crooked sign reading "Snow Cones". I hustle over, and standing behind the counter is a tall scrawny man. He appears young, with green alert eyes and a blond comb over. He is wearing a red polo t-shirt and khaki pants with a name tag that reads "Fred" pined to the middle of his shirt. The stand is the same colors as the wall, causing him to blend in with the room.

I force a smile onto my face. "Hi, Fred, how much are your snow cones?"

Fred's smile reminds me of a politician. "Why, young lady, you only have to confess all the sins you committed that landed you in Hell, and I will give you as many as you want."

"And why would you care about what I did to end up here?" I ask, suspicious.

With his slimy politician smile spreading, Fred snickers. "Young lady, I couldn't care less why you are in Hell. But those children can't hear you until you tell me what you did. Think of it as helping yourself. Or you can go join the other brainless idiots calling out to children that are deaf to them."

Resentment burns through my being, my rage building. How dare this balding man make demands from me? My entire body tightly coiled, I hiss, "I murdered twenty men over the last five years. I need ten snow cones!"

"Did you really think that would be enough? I need more details before I bestow any of my snow cones." The glee in his tone has my hands clenching.

"Fine! You want details?" I scream, my chest heaving. "I convinced twenty different men that I would fuck them. Like the pathetic little morons they were, they jumped at the chance for another notch in their bedpost. When we got to my car, I offered them a drink laced with Mexican Valium, then I drove them to an abandoned gas station, and that is where I killed them." I can feel the angry flush staining my face.

His smile stretches even further, pleased by what I have admitted. Giggling he responds, "How did you kill them?"

Now in a full-blown rage, I scream, "I stabbed some of them. I branded most of them. I tied up one dickhead and lit him on fire. Others I choked." My entire body is trembling with the urge to jump this counter and slam Fred's head on the shiny metal surface over and over until his blood coats his rundown cart and myself and his body stops twitching from the pain. My tight voice barely audible through my clench teeth I snap, "Give me the snow cones."

Fred is bent over, laughing hysterically. His entire body is shaking with his mirth. Gripping the counter, he hauls himself upright. Gasping, he croaks, "Give me a minute and you can have the cold treat." It takes him a couple of minutes to calm himself enough to fill my order. Still occasionally laughing, he hands me a tray with ten plain snow cones.

Barely calm, I snarl, "Where is the flavor?"

"You have to add juice to them yourself," he coughs.

Turning on my heel I stomp back to my assigned table. The other adults are still calling out to their shadows, while the shadows are still running, laughing and screaming at the tops of their little lungs.

Slamming the tray of snow cones down onto the vomit-colored table cloth, I snatch up the jug of berry juice, and with a violent twist of my wrist the top flies off and the purple juice drenches the front of my outfit. My eye twitches as I take a spoon and drizzle some of the juice on the flavorless snow cones. Finishing my task, I grab the tray and head back into the jumbled mess of the other prisoners and shadow children running around.

Holding the tray out as an offering for the demons I am supposed to be entertaining, I yell, "Here you little shits, I have a tasty treat for you! If you want it, go and sit back down at the table!"

"Yeah, treats!" is the response that echoes throughout the room. Pivoting to head back toward the table, my body stops as though I have hit a wall; all ten little demons are sitting at the table hands folded in front of them, completely still. Shaking myself out of my stupor I rush over before they decide to take off again. I hand out the berry-flavored snow cones before serving up juice and cake to each of the children. I take a couple of steps back, hovering over the party with the jug of juice clutched in my hands.

The shadow children are chattering and laughing hysterically amongst one another. Seeing empty cups lying on their sides I rush back over to the table, quickly snatching each cup in my hand, refilling it before setting it back down in front of the happy shadow. When all the cake has been devoured, the plates licked clean, I pass the first brightly colored wrapped package to the shadow child wearing a party hat that says "Happy Birthday". The little demon tears through the neon orange wrapping paper like a creature possessed.

The present is nothing but another shadow. All of them are, very colorful on the outside but the details are indistinguishable. The children must be able to identify the items wrapped up within, because each new item the birthday kid reveals incites additional squeals from the other children.

When all of the presents have been opened and all the juice drunk, I start cleaning up the table, taking all the trash to the fireplace to burn it. Turning back around, the shadow children and the mess I haven't cleaned up has vanished. The table resets with the same tablecloth, clean cups and plates, and a brand-new stack of presents. There are ten little shadow children sitting still like statues.

Lucifer materializes right before my eyes, posed about four feet away, cutting into my view of the table. A condescending smirk graces his face as he taunts, "What a good job you've done. Now you get to repeat the process over and over, for eternity." He paces around me, each lap circling closer and closer until he stops right behind me. His hands slowly stroke up and down my arms, his warm, moist breath tickling my ear as he whispers, "You will tell us each and every little detail, repeating them until there is nothing left inside of you but emptiness."

The shadow children spring to life, scattering throughout the room. Their little voices rise into a dull roar, mixing and amplifying the sounds of the other shadow children's screams and the party host's desperate calls for order. The warmth against my back disappears as his last words call out lovingly: "Now get back to work."

My mother was right; Hell is a never-ending child's birthday party.

When I was your age...

Lessons
from
years
past.

MICHEAL T. SMITH is a multi-genre author, typically inspirational, but he dabbles in others. He has been writing for more than twenty years, but only gained success in the last five years.

A person never knows
how their actions affect those
around them.
I learned this first hand.
It was amazing.

THE HAPPIEST DAY
OF MY LIFE

Michael T. Smith

It started innocently.

Many years ago, I worked in an office in Halifax, Nova Scotia. We had large windows that looked out over a busy overpass. I stood by one of those windows one day, when a woman in a passing car looked up and made eye contact – naturally, I waved.

A chuckle escaped my lips as she turned and tried to identify me. It was the beginning of a year of window antics. When things were slow, I stood in the window and waved at the passengers who looked up. The strange looks made me laugh – work stress was washed away.

My co-workers took an interest. They stood back, out of view, and watched the reactions I received, and laughed.

Late afternoon was the best time. Rush-hour traffic filled the overpass with cars and transit buses, and provided lots of waving material for my end-of-day routine. It didn't take long to attract a following - a group of commuters who passed the window every day and looked up at the strange waving man. There was a man with a construction truck. He'd turn on his flashing yellow lights and return my wave. There was the carpool crowd and the business lady with her children fresh from day care. My favorite was the transit bus from the docks that passed my window at 4:40 PM. It carried the same group every day. They were my biggest fans.

Waving became boring, so I devised ways to enhance my act. I made signs: "Hi!", "Hello!", "Be Happy!" I posted them in the window and waved. I stood on the window ledge in various poses, created hats from paper and file-folders, made faces, played peek-a-boo by bouncing up from below the window ledge, stuck out my tongue, tossed paper planes in the air, and once went into the walkway over the street and danced while co-workers pointed to let my fans know I was there.

Christmas approached. Job cuts were announced. Several co-workers would lose their jobs. Everyone was depressed. Stress reached a high point. We needed a miracle to break the tension.

While working a night shift, a red lab jacket attracted my attention. I picked it up and turned it in my hands. In a back corner, where packing material was kept, I used my imagination and cut thin, white sheets of cloth-like foam into strips and taped them around the cuffs and collar, down the front, and around the hem of the lab jacket. A box of foam packing and strips of tape became Santa's beard. I folded a red file folder into a hat and taped the beard to it. The whole thing slipped over my head in one piece.

The next day I hid from my co-workers, slipped into the costume, walked bravely to my desk, sat down, held my belly, and mocked Santa's chuckle. They gathered around me and laughed for the first time in weeks. A few minutes later, my supervisor walked through the door. He took three steps, looked up, saw me, paused, shook his head, turned and left.

I feared trouble. The phone on the desk rang. It was my boss. "Mike, come to my office!" I shuffled down the hall. The foam beard swished across my chest with each step.

"Come in!" The muffled voice replied to my knock. I entered and sat down. The foam on my beard creaked. He looked away from me. A bead of sweat rolled down my forehead. The only sound was the hammering of my heart.

"Mike..." That was all he managed to say. He lost his composure, leaned back in his chair, and bellowed with laughter. He held his stomach. Tears formed in his eyes, as I sat silent and confused. When he regained control, he said, "Thanks, Mike! With the job cuts, it's been hard to enjoy the Christmas season. Thanks for the laugh, I needed it."

That evening, and every evening of the Christmas season, I stood proudly in the window and waved to my fans. The bus crowd waved wildly, and the little children smiled at the strange Santa. My heart filled with joy. For a few minutes each day, we could forget the loss of jobs. I didn't know it then, but a bond was forming between my fans and I. The next spring, I discovered just how close we had become.

My wife and I were expecting our first child. I wanted the world to know. Less than a month before the birth I posted a sign in the window, "25 DAYS UNTIL 'B' DAY." My fans passed and shrugged their shoulders. The next day the sign read, "24 DAYS UNTIL 'B' DAY." Each day the number dropped, and the passing people grew more confused.

One day a sign appeared in the bus, "What is 'B' DAY?" I just waved and smiled.

Ten days before the expected date, the sign in the window read, "10 DAYS UNTIL BA-- DAY." Still the people wondered. The next day it read, "9 DAYS UNTIL BAB- DAY," then "8 DAYS UNTIL BABY DAY".

My fans finally knew what was happening. By then, my following had grown to include twenty or thirty different buses and cars. Every night they watched to see if my wife had given birth. The number decreased – excitement grew. My fans were disappointed when the count reached "zero" without an announcement. The next day the sign read, "BABY DAY 1 DAY LATE". I pretended to pull out my hair.

Each day the number changed and the interest from passing traffic grew. My wife was fourteen days overdue, before she finally went into labor. The next morning our daughter was born. I left the hospital at 5:30 AM, screamed my joy into the morning air, and drove home to sleep. I got up at noon, showered, bought cigars, and appeared at my window in time for my fans. My co-workers were ready with a banner posted in the window: "IT'S A GIRL!"

I didn't stand alone that evening. My co-workers joined me in celebration. We stood and waved our cigars in the air, as every vehicle that passed acknowledged the birth of my daughter. Finally, the bus from the docks made its turn onto the overpass and began to climb the hill. When it drew close, I climbed onto the window ledge and clasped my hands over my head in a victory pose. The bus was directly in front of me, when it stopped dead in heavy traffic, and every person on board stood with their hands in the air. Emotion choked me as I watched them celebrate my new daughter.

Then it happened: a sign popped up. It filled the windows and stretched half the length of the bus, "CONGRATULATIONS!"

Tears formed in the corners of my eyes as the bus slowly resumed its journey. I stood in silence, as it pulled from view. More fans passed. They tooted their horns or flashed their lights to congratulate me. I hardly noticed them, as I pondered what had just happened.

My daughter had been born fourteen days late. Those people must have carried that sign for weeks. Each day they must have unrolled it and then rolled it back up. The thought of them going through so much just to celebrate my new baby made me cry. I made a fool of myself for eight months. I made those people smile after a long day at work. They must have enjoyed it, because on the happiest day of my life they showed their appreciation.

That day, more than twenty years ago, changed me. I just wanted to make my day better. I didn't realize how it affected others.

Ever since then, I try to put a smile on someone's face every day. I compliment strangers on their clothing. I start conversations in elevators. I even make jokes in crowded New York City subways. Some may think I am stupid, but I know there is a chance I'm making someone's day – someone who may one day hold up a sign that says "Congratulations!"

The Fall of Life

Michael T. Smith

The nights grew longer; the air cooled; leaves changed color; migrating birds made their way south, fleeing winter. Fall was almost upon us, my favorite time of year. A walk through the forest was a trip to an art gallery. The trees compete, each a work of nature's glorious art.

A canopy of color shaded me. I stood under them, looked up and saw sunlight streaming through the branches. It struck each leaf and was reflected back with an unimaginable brilliance.

In the quiet of the forest, I heard a small snap. A single leaf floated delicately to the ground. A light breeze stirred the branches, a multicolored snow storm. The colored flakes landed on my head and shoulders. They cover the seeds and nuts dropped earlier in the year. Some already had small sprouts reaching for the sky.

The seeds of new life were soon buried under a cover of delicate and dying leaves, a cover provided by the tall trees standing over them. The leaves protected the future from the cold winter to follow. In spring, the leaves decomposed and provided rich nutrients to nourish a new generation.

A week later I was back. I wanted to enjoy the season before it was gone. The leaves rustled under my feet. The air was scented with the odor of dampness and decomposition, as the leaves began to decay, a pleasant smell. I shuffled along, pushing the leaves in front of me. They parted and swirled around my feet like the waters on a beach. My heart was heavy. Another year was gone.

At home, I looked in the mirror, a hint of grey at my temples. I noticed a few more in the whiskers on my chin and a few chest hairs followed suit. The hair on the top of my head, like the leaves, was mostly gone. I'm in the fall of life. Could my winter be close?

I sat in my chair, tried to watch a game on television, but I couldn't focus. Where did my spring and summer go?

My son walked by. He was a tall, healthy, and good looking young man. "See ya, Dad. I'm going to work." The door closed behind him.

I thought of the trees, the seeds, the nuts, the leaves, my children and grandchildren. Like the trees, I spread my seeds and protect them. They grew from seeds and sprouts, to tall, strong saplings.

The trees and I have weathered many storms. We swayed and bent under their force, but we stood over our young, sheltered them, and covered them when they were cold.

My heart felt lighter. Fall was not the beginning of the end. It is the past protecting the future. One day, a storm will blow in. I'll topple over, my winter. The young I sheltered, free of my shadow, will take my place to protect the next generation, my job complete.

Raising children causes us
to look back on one mom's life
at that age as a way to assist her son
through a difficult time.

Thirteen Again

Merri Halma

I walk out of the classroom to enter the fast moving sea of legs rushing to their next class. To a thirteen year old who only stands four foot nine, or less, the fast moving taller kids are quite intimidating because they are either too busy talking to their friends or not paying attention to the shorter kids in class. I hold my books close to my body and do my best to avoid being knocked into a wall or having another person run into me. Though thoughts become things, so someone does run into me, causing me to drop a book. I bend down to pick it up, only to have a taller student trip over me. He cusses me out, and I feel worse than I already did. The bell rings and I'm nowhere close to my next class room. I apologize as best as I can, but he hurries on. I can tell by how tall he is he is likely a ninth grader who looks down on all students in the lower grades, both literally and figuratively, since he stood at least five foot five already and was still growing.

That was over thirty, almost forty, years ago.

A thirteen year old wants to have friends, to belong and to be liked for who they are. Their body and views are changing at a rapid pace, and few really know what they want. How do we help our thirteen year olds adjust to these years?

My thirteen year told me I didn't understand what it was like walking in the hallway in his school, what it was like being jostled and pushed about. His school hallways are a mess because the bullies appear to run the hallways between classes and purposely run into kids they don't like. My son stands a bit taller than the bullies that try to run over him, but that does not keep them from being intimidating or trying to hurt him. My son was in tears, almost, as he recited his fears.

"You are taller than me, James. Imagine what it was like for me, being one of the shortest kids in my school, walking into a hallway between classes. All I could see was legs."

His expression changed a bit.

A thirteen year old wants friends, to belong, to make a difference and to know they are okay. The insecurity can grow faster than an instant message if the proper seeds are not planted by adults. To a child who is viewed as different, they become a target to those who feel they are the leaders and much tougher. My son can count all his friends, both the friends at his gaming sites and at school: his total is twenty-three. I said when I was his age my friends numbered much less.

I came home to an empty house. Even if my Mom was there it still felt empty to me because I couldn't talk to her about the torment I suffered at school. I was teased for being short, for speaking with an impediment and for my funny last name. I was afraid of what I could be and what I wanted to be. I wanted to be a writer and my Mom was afraid of my goals, too. Mostly I could not be myself. I had to hide who I was. My relationship had to be with myself, yet for too long I hide my talents. When I offered to share my writing, I was told that I had talent by some and told I didn't have talent by others. I had to find the go between.

When we view relationships, we often think of them as only relationships with other people. What about being able to bond with one's self? A healthy self concept is what so many teenagers need. I tell my son this, too. He gets this look of, "Really, Mom? I don't see how *that* could help me make friends."

I told him that when we like ourselves what another person does to hurt us will not affect us as bad. The other important relationship is to have a strong Spiritual center. To know firmly that Spirit, however you view Him or Her, is firmly on your side and inside yourself, that nothing can bother you unless you allow it to.

Teens who do not have a strong sense of self usually fall for any group or friendship that gives them big promises of becoming more than they are, power and authority even if it leads to life of crime. Instead, I give my son a sense of belonging through the church we joined. Hoping he will learn to rely on the spirituality the teen group is teaching him and hoping he will learn he can talk to me about anything and I will listen to him with an open mind, even if I don't always understand or like what I hear.

The thirteen year old that is still inside of me dares to poke her head out to look at the world around her now. "Wow," she exclaims, "those kids are not as tall as I thought they were. I am safe. I am loved. I am okay. It is okay to be who I am born to be."

A bird's eye view
of looking at one's self
as others see her.

My Life

Merri Halma, 2011

See that speck of dust? It is just a normal everyday speck of dust moving about freely. We are looking at it way above the atmosphere, as if we are looking through a microscope. There are millions of dust particles in the atmosphere. Most gravitate towards others, ending up in one central pile on top of your mother's unused figurines that you aren't supposed to touch because they are priceless and very breakable. Yet you still have an incurable desire to pick them up for a closer look and to see exactly what it is she sees in those porcelain figures of a boy with an old fashion strap around his school books in one hand and an apple for his teacher in the other. He appears to be in mid-stride and singing a happy song. Has anyone ever been that happy to be going to school?

Okay, I digress. Back to this speck of dust. We zoom in for a closer look. Metaphysicians and spiritual philosophers around the world state we are all of one mind, one consciousness. It is an illusion to be alone. Millions of people rush around from one place to another, eager to talk with their BFFs about every detail of their life.

That speck of dust becomes bigger as we get closer. We see it is not a speck of dust, but it is a person. A person alone, except for the a white cat with orange ears and orange mixed into his fur sitting in a brown overstuffed recliner adjacent from where she sits at a TV tray with a laptop on it, busy typing. Okay, the cat was just kicked out his place by the husband.

I mull around in the society of life feeling alone, feeling like I am not like others, anxious to know and believe they are okay. One isn't supposed to look too closely inside oneself nor admit all I am supposed to say. But I dare say it and dare to be ridiculed.

We are all alone.

We are alone inside the body, like a trapped animal. Our soul lives there in the persona that we have created since babyhood, raised by two or sometimes one parent and suffer the slings and arrows of our peer group. If one is vulnerable, we take on the fears and abnormal thought patterns of those around us. Kids may call us freaks or decide to make of us because we do not conform to the social norm of the day.

Permit me, if you may, to speak on the misfortune that is my life. My life of feeling isolated, alone, without a 'god' that is outside of myself, alone without close friends who actually understand me (speaking in the far time of two years and more ago). Alone in my skin feeling like I would never bond with people. Indeed, maybe it is all a lie I tell myself so I will continue hiding in my little house that is below a cement factory. Who am I to say the universe is a liar when I hear I will be a better person by embracing the pure love that is within me, when all I feel inside is hurt and isolation when I try to make new friends but am greeted with a cold shoulder because the gals really are not interested in me? I am not sure why. Am I too quiet? Am I really not their type? I want to exclude myself, but I am not willing to do that.

Social butterflies flirt and flit around, talking in excited whispers at the same time and giggle together. Take me, a listener and one who talks slow and often has to stop to correct what I say because the wrong words tend to stumble out or I stutter and trip over each syllable. Deep down, I sense they really are not interested in me. Me? I relate differently to my world. I have never felt the acceptance they have. Nor have I had a successful career that has given me rich rewards in my life. I hold myself back, trying to suppress the emotions I feel and not show that which I want to say.

Am I okay? Do you understand that I tell the truth? Do you understand that the way I talk is who I am, yet I am speaking my truth: I just have a speech impediment or language problem. Yes, I say the wrong words. Yes some of the words that tumble out of my mouth are not the right words, and I am searching for the right ones, that does not mean I am changing my story. It just means you need to be understanding of me. I want to belong. I want to be part of your social organization. Are you willing to actually get to know me, look beyond my outward clumsiness to accept me? Or will you shun me like so many people before you? Shun me because I do not fit into the social type of your organization. You wish to judge me and render me not good enough, render me inferior and toss me to the side because I am not bubbly and eager to exchange light conversation. Please, ignore me all you want. I have my own thoughts to occupy me.

If were to confess to someone my fears of rejection, it will be turned on me. I will be told I am rejecting myself. I am the one who feels the need to criticize myself and project it out onto my world, who in turn accepts my view of myself so they reflect it back to me.

Ah, the irony. The sweet, sweet taste of rusty, dusty irony. I sense so deeply that others see me as a liar because of the way my mind works and because I overcompensate for my active mind by dulling down my emotions, becoming quiet, reserved and appearing depressed when I am the opposite. When I show my aliveness, eyes beaming with joy and excitement, my mind is running on a hundred channels at once and no one can keep track of the many topics I may speak on yet it is rich with such a deepness of thought and often I get my words out of place or I jump around too much, losing the listener in the process. I also may skip details that I was sure I put in. I have had people tell me they don't believe me. I have had people look at me with anger in their eyes when I have to correct myself, even when calm.

I do my best to be a truthful person, yet it gnaws at me to my very core to sense that people do not believe me. I want to be understood. I want to be celebrated and told I have something positive to offer others. Instead, I am treated with disregard, told I can't write and I should not try to (one of my sorority sisters said that to me). I see the difference in how I am treated. People for the most part are phony, saying they care about me, showing excitement to see me when they rather not be near me, rolling their eyes. I am a new pledge, but I know I won't last long. I will not be given a chance to be accepted because I cannot become something I am not.

After outings with a group, there was ten of us. Five went one way, and three went another way. One stayed with me for a bit, but soon I was alone. I enjoyed myself but had to admit I felt abandoned. I felt left out and like I really should have stayed home. I enjoyed looking at the farmer's market and knowing I could see so much richness there. Yet deep inside, I knew I had nothing in common with these women who have known each other for thirty or forty years. The other new pledges joined in and have been richly accepted because they have rich stories to share about their families and their work. I have nothing the like to share since I work. All the spiritual philosophies I follow say as one thinks, so it will be. I know I have more to give others, yet I don't see the world responding to that.

Okay, okay, I see myself as limited. I see myself as unable to respond to that which I really would like to be. I approach businesses to talk with them and I fear I will not be heard or believed. I fear my words will come out in halting stammers and hesitations.

In my mind's eye, I want to approach each person and ask them how they see me. I want to know if they see me as believable. Okay, I admit I hide my true self from the world. I give off the air that I am a dull person, and not very interesting. I am not being real.

I hide in my house for the most part. I hide because I know it is a safer world. I hide. I joined the sorority to find acceptance and hopefully find something I have been longing for a long time: good friends who will always be there for me. Instead, I feel more isolated and rebuffed. I am not part of them.

That takes us back to the speck of dust. That is me, wanting to be a part of a group. You see that speck of dust, how it sits alone on the Mahogany table? It is alone, sitting on an office chair with a TV tray in front of it. On the TV tray is a laptop computer and it is busy writing about a world much larger than her which also surrounds her. Other dust particles gather together, join as one large dust bunny, and float off to travel under the couch or attach themselves to the white and orange cat, that is now back on the recliner, curled up to sleep. The dust particle looks up and sees me, it recognizes we are the same, longing to be part of the that dust bunny that is off having larger adventures outside of the small world in which it lives. It lives in self pity: it wishes to abandon the self pity. It longs to embrace a world that is friendly and accepts all people, including her, no matter how she relates to herself.

OUT OF THIS WORLD

Adventures through space and time.

S.C. FANTOZZI lives and works in Idaho. She is a landscaper, horsewoman, and avid rock hound. Her home is shared by her dog, seven cats, and flock of chickens and ducks.

WATER, WATER

S.C. Fantozzi

No one knew when the heat was going to break. The scientists who had warned of global warming for years merely bowed their heads as the world boiled alive, the average man finally taking notice of the chaos descending across the earth.

The raging heat wave scorched the western U.S. until fires raged across the landscape, gutting the sagebrush and mountain ranges, black dirt stretching for miles. Firemen fought the blazes and people evacuated their homes, as states of emergency were declared across the United States from Texas to Idaho. The sky remained clear for months on end, the forecast of rain never an option for scape-goated local weather men.

Some cities tried cloud seeding and others brought in shamans, each municipality hoping to find a solution to the blazing heat. Nothing worked. Schools were cancelled, crops began to fail and people were advised to stay inside. On the verge of nationwide panic, the country needed a miracle.

And one day, it started to rain.

The storms weren't part of the regular weather patterns that swept in from the Pacific Ocean, nor were they byproducts of El Nino or the Gulf of Mexico. Something new had arrived on the gusting winds, and regardless of the origin, the chain of rainfalls quenched the burning fires, water cascading from the heavens in buckets, skies black with heavy clouds and land soaked through with torrents of moisture.

For a while, the world breathed a sigh of relief. Many thought the worst was over, and by all accounts, it was. Cities got back to work, weary firemen returned home, and the skies cleared of the smoke that had obscured the sun for weeks.

But the rain didn't stop.

At first it was merely a curiosity, a particularly long weather system that hovered for days, dumping more rain on the deserts than had been seen in decades. Rivers ran high, dry lakes filled and children danced in the torrential downpour. The meteorological community was intrigued, but no alarms went off.

Then the storm moved east, hammering the Midwest and the eastern seaboard, giving the west coast a well-deserved reprieve.

For three days.

Those days, those three little days, would be remembered by those who survived the coming years as the last time things were ever normal. People would talk about those three days like they were a dream, something so far removed from reality that it was almost sacred. A picnic, birthdays, even walking the dog was cause enough for a story or a memory.

The sunset on the third day burned red, clouds looming on the far horizon as the sky flashed in gold and bronze.

It was the final night the world remembered color.

≈ ≈ ≈ ≈ ≈

Kay Martinelli spent those three days like the two months before it, staring out at cold stone brick from behind the walls of her prison cell. The rain had kept the population inside for the week previous, and when the sun had finally emerged from behind the cloud cover even her normally dour spirits had been lifted.

Kay didn't often think about those days, in the time before everything had gone to hell. She'd loathed prison with a fiery passion, but sometimes, in the darkest part of the night when she was curled up in a corner alone, sopping wet and miserable, she wished for the thick stone walls and strict routine that had governed her days.

After those three days, everything had fallen apart.

The rain returned on the fourth morning, and it didn't stop. One week turned into two, and then weeks blurred into months. Rain poured from the sky in seemingly endless sheets, flooding low lying towns and sweeping away others entirely. Sometimes it was thunderstorms, other days a light drizzle.

But always it rained.

It was a nationwide crisis the likes of which the country had never seen. State governments were overwhelmed and local first responders could do little but order people to evacuate to higher ground.

Before long, it became apparent that something had gone horribly wrong with Mother Nature. A rage burned in her soul, bright despite the endless clouds and drizzle. The reckoning had come, but not at the hands of the Horsemen or the media. As the water pooled and the seas rose, no one knew how bad it was really going to get.

Not until the mist began to form.

The United States was drowning and the rest of the world was close behind. After the third month of incessant rain, several countries closest to the equator lost contact with the rest of the world. No one could spare the time or the money to find out why, not when the global crisis reached apocalyptic levels. Religious leaders preached to their congregations, governments tried in vain to keep their citizens together, and scientists scrambled to document the raging weather that seemed intent on washing the human race from the face of the planet. Kay thought it was all a load of shit.

It wasn't until reports of monsters began to float in that the panic began in earnest. At first, the stories were seen as tasteless jokes, nothing more than a media scam intended to cause even more trouble. When hazy film footage began to float over what little infrastructure was left, Kay finally gathered with the other prisoners to watch the misty pictures on the little television in the lounge. The accounts made a trail, tracking up from South America along the shores of the oceans, whispers of dark terrors that seemed too fanciful to be real.

The power went down, and after twenty-four hours, Kay walked out of prison a free woman. Shivering, she stood on the darkened street, the sidewalks deserted, gutters running with rivers. Something in her gut told her that there was going to be no recovery, and for the first time, she felt the first hints of misgiving. The rain plastered her hair to her skull as she looked up into the black afternoon sky, mist curling around her ankles. When the U.S. lost contact with its neighbor to the south, the military was mustered for a final stand.

After that, it really was a matter of history.

≈≈≈≈≈

Six Years after the Rains...

Kay crept through the swamp with one hand on her knife, the other resting on the edge of her holstered .9mm. One could never be too careful when traversing the edges of the Mist. Sometimes her hunt was successful, and other times she came back with nothing more than wet shoes and a bad attitude. The sound of a quail echoing through the brush made her stop, and she tilted her head, tucking her long leather coat tighter around her waist before she began to move again.

What had once been desert had since become a western Everglades, omnipresent mist hovering low and thick against the ground. It was late enough to be called early, and the white fog reflected the muted light of the moon above, casting inky shadows and strange nebulous glints of silver. The flashlight in her hand danced through the ever present spit of water from above and Kay glanced once again at the alien landscape around her.

The snap of a stick made her pause once again, peering through the forest of rotting junipers as best she could. The blackened trees hung low in the water that lapped below the ankles of her waterproof boots, algae and who knew what else clinging to slowly decaying trunks. The branches were nearly bare, long lost needles rotted to nothing, the wood turning black and sloughing off as the rains stripped the trees where they stood. Despite the cloud cover, the air rang cold, the temperate winters of the high desert managing to hang on a little longer as swampland reclaimed the territory lost by the ancient seas.

Kay's mane of golden hair was the only thing for miles with any semblance of color, and the waterfall between her shoulder blades reflected in the puddles around her, the water catching a glimpse of yellow before silver and black reclaimed the pools.

It was late, and she was beyond tired, but with a mile to go before she would be out of the forest and back to her latest camp, she carried on. It had been a bad idea to go out in the first place, but breaks in the rain were few and far between and she'd decided it was worth the chance.

Something that decidedly wasn't a quail growled somewhere off to her left, the cloying stench reaching her nose just as her heart kicked into double time. Crouching low, she froze, eyes straining to see as she clicked the flashlight off. Her gun was in her hand before she knew it and just as she managed to pinpoint the general direction of the noise, something else moved behind her.

The figure that pressed against her side was not one of the writhing creatures that stalked the swamps, but she stiffened anyway as the familiar form shoved her to the ground, half submerging both of them in the sticky black mud that drifted just under the water.

Kay knew that something was up, so she didn't protest the manhandling.

"Daniel."

"Hold still," he muttered back. "There's a bunch coming."

Kay nodded, trying to breathe as shallowly as possible to avoid the misting breath that would give away their position.

Neither moved for a long time, but they heard the sloughing footsteps of their pursuers, accompanied by the low guttural moans and snarls that seemed to always follow the larger packs.

Kay caught a glimpse of the herd as it passed, and though she'd arguably seen worse, the living nightmares never failed to send a shiver through her. Crouched figures moving almost as one, twisted spines and decaying musculature contorting the bodies into parodies of life. Flesh slowly turned to gelatinous pus and faces sagged into perpetual frowns, long noses always searching for prey. Not many things in life frightened Kay. She'd been through foster homes, prison, and a number of unsavory situations that had nothing to do with the apocalypse.

But she'd never signed up for monsters.

As the creatures moved past, Kay tried not to look into the burning black eyes that seemed to stare back at her even through the inky night.

She hated those eyes. Hated that the few times she'd been close to them, she'd seen her own reflection staring back at her.

Nothing moved for a long few minutes, and when the sounds finally faded into the distance Daniel nudged her on the back, forcing her to move. By the time they'd righted themselves, they were both shivering and covered in black mud. Kay was not at all amused.

"Move it," she hissed, giving her compatriot a shove when he opened his mouth. "They might be coming back."

"What the hell are you doing out here in the first place?" Daniel shot back, beginning to work on pulling his feet from the suction of the muddy swamp.

"Nothing you need to concern yourself with," Kay replied, wondering how he always managed to bring out the argumentative side of her.

Granted, nearly all her sides were argumentative, but that was beside the point.

"You're going to get yourself killed," he admonished, finally working his feet free. "That was a close call even for you."

Steadfastly ignoring her companion, Kay splashed her way towards home. It was an old argument between them and she was certain they'd rehash the ground again. For the moment, however, she concentrated on leading them through the last of the juniper forest and onto the high ground of the foothills. That was the only nice thing about the west. While there were plenty of valleys and gorges for the water to congregate in, there were just as many mountains and hills where the land retained its last feeble hold against the swamps. Their little slice of hell was located on the side of one such relatively steep hill that jutted out from the edge of a larger mountain. The natural cave system didn't recede back very far, but it was made of solid rock, and a little creative redecorating from Kay and her stash of explosives had hollowed out an area roughly the size of a typical master bedroom; small for her liking, but doable.

≈≈≈≈≈

Daniel huffed out another breath as the toe of his boot caught on a hidden rock, sighing in relief as the terrain began to slope upwards, the water falling behind them. Watching Kay climb the hill in front of him, he tried not to be too irritated at her blatant disregard for safety. He'd figured out early on in their reluctant partnership that she was more at home at the end of the world than he would ever be. Despite the rain and the monsters and everything else that came along with it, Kay carried on as if she were merely out for an afternoon walk.

He wasn't like that. His family, his friends, all of them had perished in the floods. Daniel didn't like fighting, but somehow, it had become his life's work. He had learned, and while he'd never be as proficient as Kay, he could hold his own. After the five years they'd spent together, Daniel really didn't know much about his roommate, although she'd saved his life when everything had first gone to hell. She didn't talk about her past and he had never felt confident enough to ask her about it. He'd seen the tattoos on her back though, the sweeping lines covering white scars that ran in thin lines across her shoulders.

Whatever life she'd lived before their paths had crossed, it certainly hadn't been a pleasant one.

"Hurry up," Kay hissed, breaking him from his thoughts. He'd fallen back, and sucked in another lungful of humid air as he doubled his efforts to climb the ever-steepening incline.

Kay raised her head to the sky, the clouds taking on the first dingy tint of blue that signified the coming morning. "The sun's going to be up soon."

Daylight no longer meant a sanctuary from the evils of the world. Instead, it just made it harder to stay hidden, though the sun would barely penetrate the perpetual cloud layer. Daniel let his own face drift to the sky, unsurprised when he felt the teardrop of moisture land on his cheek. Kay caught his gaze for a moment, something flashing across the pale green of her eyes, as though she knew exactly what he was thinking. Shrugging, she turned and headed back up the hill.

Daniel sighed, following after her. The clouds overhead boiled in agitation, the few faint stars fading as the gray morning mist thickened like pastry dough. The weeping world spun on, the breaking day just like all the others: wet, cold and so, so quiet.

And of course, it was going to rain.

Space Worms

S.C. Fantozzi

C harlotte wasn't a screamer, but when she stepped into the corridor outside her bunk and saw a three inch, slime-covered worm crawling across the deck, she wasn't ashamed that she let out a small yip of displeasure. Then again, it might have been more than just a yip, as a moment later the door next to her's slammed open and Jasper came stumbling out, shirtless, disheveled, and brandishing a shock gun.

"What the hell, Charlotte?" He said. "I thought we were under attack!" He blinked the sleep out of his eyes and glanced up and down the ship's deserted corridor. "Why are you shouting?"

Charlotte merely folded her arms across her chest and nodded at the floor, where the intrepid little worm was nearing the junction where steel plated deck met wall.

Jasper's eyes fixed on the creature like it was the Devil himself. His foot slammed down without a moment's hesitation. The impact was firm and final, an unpleasant squashing noise and foul odor filling the air as the worm burst into a puddle of steaming ooze.

"That was disgusting," Charlotte said, taking a quick step back and wrinkling her nose at the stench. Jasper didn't reply, his eyes quickly clearing of the haze of sleep, narrowing as he clutched the shock gun even harder. He strode across the hall to a small speaker inset in the wall, ignoring the slime trail he left under his left foot and Charlotte's slowly raising eyebrow. She watched in amusement as he stabbed the intercom button harder than necessary. "Crash, if you're not already, get up."

"Captain…" the hissing voice came echoing through the tiny speaker almost immediately. The ship's notoriously recalcitrant mechanic had a distinct tremor to his heavily accented voice. "We have a problem. Worms."

"I'm aware of that," Jasper said, banging his forehead against the wall. "How bad?"

"Not good."

Charlotte shook her head at Crash's typical vagueness, glancing down the hall towards the kitchen as she listened in on Jasper's conversation.

"Fix it," Jasper ordered. "I don't care if you have to vent the ship. Get them out."

"Yes sir." The intercom clicked off and Jasper turned to stare at Charlotte, hair standing up like a crowd of worshipers in front of an idol. "What time is it?"

"Almost five," she replied.

He groaned and ran a hand across his face. "Why the hell are you even awake?"

She shrugged. "I was going for a little workout." She glanced down at the murder scene. "Guess that plan's out."

Jasper yawned and shook his head. "There's something wrong with you. You don't sleep enough."

Charlotte just smirked. "I'd say you have bigger problems than my sleep schedule."

Jasper stood and stared half-dressed, green slime seeping through his toes. She suppressed a laugh with extreme effort.

"We've got to get them out." Jasper gestured with the weapon he still held in his left hand. "The last time this happened it took months. They were everywhere—in the food, the showers. Hell, Crash was pulling them out of the star drive."

"You're not the first ship to have worms," Charlotte said. "We'll get them one way or another." She paused. "But if you're planning to go on a killing spree this morning, you might want to get some shoes on first."

For the first time, Jasper seemed to realize the show he was putting on, talking to his first officer about massacring worms in just his ratty sweats. Sighing, he figured it was far from the strangest conversation they'd ever had.

A squelch from above and they both looked up. Jasper groaned as another bundle of green slime began to wriggle out of one of the overhead ducts, undisturbed by his glare. Charlotte crossed her arms over her chest, watching as a second worm managed to free itself and plummet to the deck, body exploding with enough force to send chunks of flesh all over the lower portion of the walls.

Feeling her eye start to twitch, Charlotte tried to keep a straight face as Jasper turned his expression to her. "It's not funny," he said.

She settled for a slight grin. "Just a little bit."

"You won't be saying that when you wake up in the middle of the night with a slime trail across your forehead."

A high pitched scream echoed from the direction of the dining area, followed by the sound of breaking china. Jasper made a sound she'd only heard from prisoners facing the death sentence.

"Cheer up," Charlotte said, slapping him on the shoulder as she slipped past, careful to avoid the pools of slime as she walked.

"If you say things can't get any worse, I'm venting you along with the worms," he hollered after her.

Charlotte grinned as she headed for the galley. "You should know by now that things can always get worse."

Jasper shook his head. "Great."

Charlotte just laughed.

ANDREW MAJORS lives in Nampa, Idaho. Apart from this collection, he has been recently published in a fantasy anthology by Tuscany Bay Books, and is looking to secure further work in the future in between bouts of unemployment.

He greatly appreciates the Caldwell Writers Club for their love and support.

Children can be rather impressionable,
so it's important to have good role models.

Veil of the Crimson Knight

Andrew Majors

Samath was five when he discovered what he wished to be. It happened on a visit with his parents to Arionath, City of the High Hill, whose towers were granite and white marble, and whose streets were filthy cobblestone. It was there he saw his first robbery, and his first execution.

The old man was weak, but his screams were strong enough to draw the crowd's attention to the thief as he ran, knocking over merchant booths as he went. It was only later Samath realized—much later—why the crowd leapt away from the man as if he were sick with the plague. They wanted to give his pursuer the widest possible berth.

He saw everything from his mother's arms, while she and his father cowered beneath their table in the market-place's far corner. It started with a faint, ruddy glow. A kind of mist poured into the open air from everyplace: up from the street, out of open doors, from the alleyways and the sewer, coalescing into a thin red cloud which held within it the shape of a man. That man held in his hands a halberd of prodigious length and size. Gripping it in two murky hands, he swung, blade cleaving the air fast as a stroke of lightning. Samath's eyes were covered by his mother's hand the instant after he saw the thief's head split like a rotten watermelon.

After the screams subsided and the blood dried, the market returned to peace. Samath's father made enough money that day to buy him a small wooden knight from a toy seller. They returned to the village a week earlier than planned, partly due to his mother's begging and partly because they had sold most of their crop. When they got home Samath painted the knight bright red.

Seventeen years passed. Samath began working the family plot, began to smoke (whenever he could lift the pipe from his father's bag), had his first fight, his first drink, his first girl in the orchard off the main road, and lost his mother to the grippe. In all that time he kept the knight with him, on his bed and, when he grew too old for it, in a wooden box behind a stone in the garden wall. If you asked him why he could not explain, only that it pleased him to do so. A strange plan had begun to form in his mind, the particulars of which he would never tell anyone, not even his father.

When his labors for the day were done he would ride for town, and in the tavern and the square he would listen for talk of Arionath. He heard many things, but the exploits of the Crimson Knight—of which little was spoken—he never forgot. It was by chance one day he overheard the wizard's apprentice drowning himself in a stein while rambling about a tamed demon. With most of his money, a few more steins and a grimoire stolen from the man's satchel, Samath managed to approximate something of the truth:

"...Chained an' made 'elpless, servin' the downtrodden an' weak (deadly saints that's good). He's the Ward of Arionath's e'ermore. Defends the city from those who shirk the law—a lil' more if you please, that's the stuff—an' once summoned e' can't be killed, delayed or bought off till he finds his quarry an' absorbs the essence to his being. Say, you folk have any 'o those ales what are made from lingonberry?"

When his father passed Samath sold the farm, taking nothing with him save the clothes on his back, a long, thin dagger his grandsire had bartered away from some fellow soldier in the wars, and the toy knight. He took the horse to Reed's Gate and sold it, and with the money bought passage into Arionath. Before long he stood in the marketplace where he had once watched the Knight work. In one hand he held the dagger.

His first victim was a row of ripe cantaloupes. Ignoring the merchant's cries he plunged it into them again and again. He went up and down the rows of stalls, overturning them, clearing tables and throwing their contents at passersby, shouting that the Ward was a usurper, the Captain of the Guard a fatheaded fool and both their wives whores.

The Knight soon stood before him. Samath held the dagger at his side and watched the diaphanous cloud approach, halberd tight in his misty hands. He heard a low purr in his ears, the sound of a tiger in the brush, and within the curling red mist he saw, lidless and glaring, a pair of deep yellow eyes taunting him with the grim prospect of eternity.

He looked into them, and sheathed his dagger. The halberd struck quick and clean.

For a long time after—till the last Ward abdicated the throne, till the city's walls were pebbles and its very name was forgotten—the Knight did his job. In the latter days went dark rumors concerning those whose crimes were heinous beyond measure. It was said the cloud of the Knight took a special form for them: a young man with a long dagger, whose kills were slow and torturous and done with exceeding devotion. Even now, on dark nights when the moon is new and the wind is still, it is said on that desolate hill where grand Arionath once stood, evil men may cower yet at the deathly veil of the Crimson Knight.

Inside the Forgotten Church

S.C. Fantozzi

C alamity was calling, but no one answered.

No one ever answered her. Not during the days and certainly not during the dark nights when she was left alone in the cold, wandering like the ghost so many accused her of being. Maybe there were spirits following her, but just like the incessant flow of time, they never stopped long enough to present themselves.

Calamity walked, steps as sure as they'd been all those years before, when her back had been straight and her hair the same hue as a corn harvest. The hall of worship with its tall, stained glass angels looked down upon her as she shuffled up the center aisle, hands weathered and worn and so, so cold.

It was always cold.

She'd never been much for religion, but in the end, after she'd wandered further than she'd ever thought possible, her final shelter had been in the carcass of an old stone church, the drafty rooms dust-filled and damp. Even though she was rotting away right along with her home, she liked to believe that she still claimed some of the same grace and grandeur that the old structure had once possessed.

The pews that flanked her were dry-rotted and dusty, and as she approached the altar she hesitated, shadows casts like feathers across the front row. Head held up, Calamity let her eyes fall to the left, just like they always did, onto the massive stained glass window overhead, filthy but unbroken; she let a small smile drift to her pale lips.

In the front row, just like always, sat Michael.

She said nothing as she took her place beside him. The evening light was fading, the night wind moaning with a perspicacity that spoke of great things to come. Calamity watched the faint colors cast by the rainbow glass as they splashed the walls, shades of gold and green and violet blending together until the world seemed to forget what dark horrors lurked in the shadows.

Sometimes, she wished for the demons of hell, for the devil, for something other than the empty church where she and Michael sat, year after year. With each dull thud in her chest, the wood and stone around her seemed to echo until there may as well have been a drum beating inside her very skull.

"My darling," Calamity spoke quietly, watching the dark and cobweb covered candles that still littered God's stage. "I do believe those spiders are going to make their nests in our bones."

Michael didn't reply.

Calamity ran a hand over the hollow of her throat, where her collar bones pressed against her skin like angel wings, a moment of divinity trapped within a rotting mortal form. Sighing, she bowed her head in a mockery of prayer before she finally pushed herself back to her feet.

"Michael," she said softly. "I think it's time to be going now."

She'd said the words a hundred times before, but he never moved from his spot, arms draped at his sides, head tilted up as though in witness to the grace of God.

Calamity shook her own head, coming to a stop before him. Leaning down, she looked into his once proud face, now barely more than a laughing skull, with dark, hollow eye sockets and weathered bone. She'd loved him once. At least, she'd thought it was love.

"We were young," she told him, patting one hand against his skeletal fingers. "And beautiful."

And they'd intended to stay that way, so emboldened by passion that they'd deemed it better to die at their own hand, in a moment of their choosing, than to waste away into old age.

A lover's pact, they had called it, confirmed in front of the Lord as they'd plunged daggers into their chests.

Or, at least Michael had.

Calamity had watched him die, seen the betrayal in his gaze as his blade had clattered to the floor, the red so brilliant it had almost taken her breath away. She remembered the coppery scent and the feel of it on her hands as she'd watched the last of his life drain away, leaving nothing behind but a shell.

It had been the perfect plan.

Until she'd been trapped.

"It seems I underestimated you, dear," Calamity told the skull, one desiccated hand cradling her chin in thought. She'd never figured out what magic he'd used to hold her there, to keep her trapped within the holy house, forever at his side, but as the years had passed, she'd forgiven him for it.

Outside, wars raged, plagues killed millions and religions rose and fell like the tides, but she remained. Always fading, her skin dulling a little more with each passing sun, always wondering when she too, would cease to be trapped in her own private hell.

Slowly, Calamity leaned forward, pressing her lips against the rough bone of her lover, recalling a day when the action would have filled her with fire. Now, it merely served to remind her of what she could no longer possess.

"Until tomorrow," she said, pulling away to begin the long walk back down the aisle.

Outside, as night fell, the church sat as it had for years: four walls and a roof. It was where people had come to celebrate, to mourn, to hope and to cry. The bricks had weathered with time, the tapestries frayed and at the end of it all, there was no one left to ask forgiveness, or to seek guidance.

None but the two specters, whose hearts sat, dried and broken, like the shards of so much stained glass, on the dark and dusty floor.

Merely to belong
is often the highest aspiration
of the unhappy.

The Oraculists of Oribiro

Andrew Majors

The sun sank, turning the seaway to a thin trough of gold, casting long shadows from the mangrove trunks with their jagged black roots that bowed low against the horizon, so he laid upon the mat, knitted his hands across his chest and, closing his eyes, let his thoughts by thin degrees turn from the world to that hidden place called Oribiro, mystic citadel in the high mountains slumbering beneath its blanket of snow and pillow of cloud, for there, deep within the great vaults of its stone undercity, strange and terrible rituals were conducted whose precious secrets he desired more than anything to know.

He dreamed them again. Thirteen monks in red cloaks, their faces hooded, stood before the ancient dais in the inner sanctum. Thin tongues of flame sputtering in torches upon the slimy walls were their only light. The monks lifted their withered hands and the ancient intonations sounded forth. The torches fell to the floor, sputtered, and died in total darkness. All around them now were the faintest impressions of a gigantic cavern, its pillars the size of cities, its roof and farthest reaches lost in murky twilight air. The floor held carven lines of every size, marking maps without number. Auras of tiny lights danced above them, shining like fireflies.

The monks now stood within that magnificent child of eternity, the final resting place of consciousness which wise men called the Wake.

And the Wake was mystery itself; no deity ever shewed there, no sorcerer claimed to have built it or lighted the way to its door, and none who ventured into the depths of its halls returned to speak of any heaven or hell beyond it. It stood as the mausoleum of all possibility, a repository of worlds without number, every soul that ever was held alike in its pitiless grip to await the passing of eternity.

He watched the monks work. Their gentlest footfalls became the volleys of a cannonade, echoing in numbed symphony against the invisible walls. Their whispers, murmurs rising in a dozen tongues, flitted like smoke from realm to realm. They were the avatars of Fate, for centuries of careful study and practice had taught them to become masters of destiny, and puppeteering the countless strings of the enthralled infinities in this weird place was

their errand, as God's absence impelled them by some unknown compact to continue His sly work.

The plays unfolded. The monks' whispers were soothing in some worlds, pitiless in others, but all directed their
charges without comment or explanation, an untold era of
work within the steady march of time. Misery, heartbreak
and shame befell a million beings. Triumph, victory and
joyous celebration touched a million more. At last they
relented, and he considered their task complete until he
watched them gather around a final world, one familiar to
him. It was laid out atop a great stone table in one of the
farthest corners of the corner-less room, its surface puls-
ing with the faded and dingy lights of mortal man.

For a long while the monks stood before it in silent
contemplation. He did not have the wherewithal to glean
their thoughts, but anticipation fluttered in him, telling
him they were deliberating, choosing a thread whose
length was of the proper ponderousness to meddle in the
affairs of this faraway place. Though surely the world of
man was too beneath their like, why else would they—?

A thin hand with pointed fingers struck the map like a
cobra. He felt a jolt of pain in one arm. His eyes snapped
open. He realized at once he was no longer alone.

The monks stood around him in a semicircle, gathered
as they had been before the stone table, their robes lurid
crimson in the dusk-light. He saw the shadowed outlines
of their hooded faces, grave countenances of inhuman
construction. The smell of dust and decay warred with the
magnolias. A grave silence overtook the rushing tongue of
the seaway and the clanging bells of the riverboats.

He tried struggling to his feet. Acting as one, they pinned him down. Terror consumed him as one monk knelt near his head. Leaning close it said, in the deathliest whisper hissed between decayed, broken teeth: "Away..."

He blinked, and the monks were gone, a night terror dissolved in memory.

He sat up, breathing heavily, grateful his encounter had been so fleeting, but as he turned the word over in his head sorrow came upon him. It was dismissal; they did not deign to share their secrets with the likes of him. He was to dream of them no more.

He left the house, and sat on the porch to watch evening come, pretending to be content as the loons cried and the ceaseless Mississippi rushed by. But in the depths of his heart he cursed his fate, dreaming awake of someday when he could leave this ill-made place and travel beyond, into the farthest worlds, and seek those places, that power and that fame which would make him worthy to glean all the secrets of the Oraculists of Oribiro.

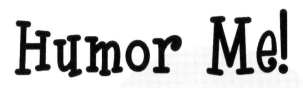

Humor Me!

Prose and poems
to tickle you pink.

STEVE PRAGER is a retired military musician and Postmaster who lives in an old cottage near downtown Caldwell, Idaho, with his lovely wife Susan. He stays busy collecting unique words, writing cheery obituaries, and trying to play jazz.

Hit the road...
just for the heck of it.

Make Your Next Weekend a "Serentripity"

Steve Prager

Ah, **the road trip!** From Steinbeck to Kerouac, from *Easy Rider* to *Little Miss Sunshine*, the classic American road trip has burned its tire marks into our nation's psyche.

We New Worlders - the'pluribus' of unum fame, the descendants of the Pilgrims and progeny of Daniel Boone and Lewis and Clark - we positively thrill to the idea of adventure on the open road. Cue up *Born to be Wild* and we can pull on a Harley Davidson t-shirt and fire up the 3D version of *Wild Hogs* before the popcorn is done.

The problem is – we don't actually go anywhere anymore.

On a trip to nowhere...

Oh sure, we travel. Disneyland, visit the grandkids, cruises; if we're lucky, maybe a timeshare in Cabo. All these are important, to be sure (love those grandkids), but maybe a little too safe and predictable.

So we log miles on the road, but they're mostly of the mind-numbing variety, `a la "I don't know how I ever had time to work because I stay so busy running errands." The odometer is spinning, but we ain't goin' nowhere, and all our busyness is hardly the spontaneous asphalt safari our forefathers (and mothers) claimed as their heritage.

How can we get away from the comfortable and familiar and reclaim that "Easy Rider" vibe? Now that outlet malls are the number one tourist destination in many states (Oregon for example), how can we flee the Starbucks nation with its homogenous strip malls and taste-a-like fast food, and experience a real, pulse-quickening adventure on the "blue highways"?

One word.

Check it out. (I wish I could say I invented it.)

Serentripity.

Serentripity (se-ren-TRIP-it-ee) n. *An adventure–filled road trip with no definite goal; serendipitous travel filled with a sense of joyous abandon.*

A Serentripity is a planned/un-planned event. All you need is a weekend to start. Back roads are preferred. Reservations are taboo because you don't know where you'll be at the end of the day.

One unknown road leads to another and to another; getting lost is being found. The journey itself is the destination, and the goal is no goal at all - except the feeling of the wind in your hair.

Running with the wind...

To get a better on grip on Serentripity and what the concept can mean, let's imagine two very different weekends for our neighbors, John and Mary:

Typical 21st century travel :

John and Mary script a familiar quick trip to a popular theme park. Loaded down with enough snacks and creature comforts to supply the *Titanic*, they fly down the interstate, entombed in their air-conditioned palace on wheels. Numb to the scenery, John and Mary's senses register only the blur of other cars and billboards; while in the backseat, the kids feast on Disney movies and sugar.

Meals consist of gobbling down freeway plasti-food; making good time is the only objective. Arriving at their destination, they hurriedly "do" the park, checking off each attraction like a man given only 24 hours to do a life's worth of bucket lists.

The return trip is a Groundhog Day in reverse; once home, they fall into bed, exhausted from their 'travel'. Sadly, their mini-vacay to Wally World was crowded, expensive, and ultimately forgettable.

Serentripity:

John and Mary have no definite plan. After the car is loaded with enough supplies for a weekend and the gas tank is filled, they set out on a local wooded highway they've always wanted to explore. When John and Mary come to a crossroads, they choose the most appealing path. When something pleases or intrigues them, they pull over and participate.

Over a single weekend, John and Mary sample roadside fruit, hike to a waterfall, get lost, discover quaint towns, sleep in a 50's themed motel, ride a ferry across a wild river, and make forever memories. And when they return home, they are refreshed, rested, and excited about their next journey.

Serendipity + your trip = Serentripity!

Born to be...

As you can see, Serentripity doesn't have a lot of rules, only suggestions. Serentripity works best with only a vague outline of a destination, a desire to wander over new roads, room to change direction at will, and time to stop and discover whatever grabs your fancy.

See the list below for a few tips on how to have a great Serentripity weekend. I'll be with you in spirit.

Full disclosure: My wife and I have taken many Serentripities over the years, including an 8,000 mile, month-long marathon from coast to coast. No one died, no animals were injured, and we only had to sleep in the car once.

Tips for a Great Serentripity Weekend

- Gas up the car completely when you begin and re-member to refuel when the gauge hits the halfway mark
- Pack snacks, plenty of water, necessary meds, and one change of underwear
- Wear your best hiking shoes
- Carry a good state map
- Bring cash for the unexpected garage sale or Satur-day market
- Avoid freeways at all costs
- Take the backroads
- Believe that small towns have the biggest stories to tell
- Be prepared to get out of the car and explore
- Leave plenty of time for unexpected discoveries

What goes through your mind
when you sit
on the porcelain thrown?

Sitting on a Toilet

SueDean Morris

Sitting on a toilet
Practically touching the wall
My legs and butt are now numb
My back wishes to relax.

My mind spins and turns
Over all my problems
My head begins to ache
No Tylenol in sight.

On my left lays
A sink that needs cleaning
Female stuff like hair crap
Takes up a lot of space.

The above toilet shelf
Gets in the way
Not very sturdy
Oh, I wish this useless stuff would vanish.

This is the end of my poem
I'm tired of the cramped space.
But I really need to stand up
To get my circulation back!

ANGELA MATLASHEVSKY is an author and illustrator that works and lives in Caldwell, Idaho. She is fond of painting and reading, as well as taking walks along the lake shore and picking wildflowers. Her work is most inspired by poetry and music, as well as her Ukrainian heritage.

* Cough, Cough *

Angela Matlashevsky

A little boy went on a walk
    And found a pile of bones.
    Unconcerned, he carried on
      'Til he heard the old bones moan.

      The boy asked, "Was that you who sighed?"
        "'Twas I," the pile of bones replied.

The boy dug through the ivory bones,
Looking for a head,
But, as it was a pile of bones,
Found a skull instead.

The boy asked, "Why the plaintive wail?"
The skull said, "I will tell my tale."

Years ago when I was young
And still a human, too,
I felt a sniffle in my nose
And caught the blasted flu.

I'd had the flu before, you know,
When I was younger still,
So I worried not and carried on
For I had time to kill.

It's just a silly flu, I thought,
And soon it will be gone.
I couldn't have known back then that I
Would be so very wrong.

A little tickle in my throat
Was how it all began.
I took a pill and went to sleep,
Expecting it to end.

When I awoke, my poor, poor throat
Had completely swollen closed.

The tickle was now behind my eyes
And up, up in my nose.

I cried for help; no cry came out.
I got up to my feet.
My head was throbbing, spinning, gnawing,
So I made a quick retreat
      back to my bed and closed my eyes
And lay my head back down.
A little longer, I told myself,
And then I'll come around.

But I didn't come around at all
And soon my mother knew
And, as mother's go, she always, always
Knew just what to do.

              Out came her book of "medicines".
               "No need to call the doctor in!"

So wrapped in blankets, maybe three,
      Turban headed, wild-thyme tea,
Poultice made of ground up ginger,
      Onion-honey-garlic tincture,
Hot baths, foot baths, powdered mustard
      Strawberry jelly, and homemade custard.

Ha! Just kidding! No sugar for you!
    Just root wine and a secret brew
        Of twigs and berries, leaves and flowers,
            Every hour, on the hour.

          "Tough break!" the little boy then said,
           "But how did you end up so dead?"

"I wasn't finished, little boy,
So please don't interrupt!"
    The skull coughed maybe once or twice
      Then shouted, "Listen up!"

A day went by, and then another,
But as if under a curse,
Not only did I fail to get better,
    I was getting even worse!

Headaches, fever, ear infection,
    Joints so stiff I couldn't walk.
Back aches, leg cramps, indigestion,
      Swollen tonsils, couldn't talk

Is this the end? I weakly pondered,
As fever chills shook up my core.
No! I refuse!
    I then decided I would not take it anymore.

And I decided then and there:
Once can't be sick if there's no one there.

"That seems a little bit extreme,"
The boy rightly deduced.
"Were you really feeling all that bad?"

"That's right," said the skull
For it was the truth.

So I first removed my eyes and nose,
And then went all my fingers and toes.
No more sensitive sight and smell!
And then I tossed my brain as well.
No more headaches, not restless dreams,
Then I pulled off my skin right at the seams.
No more un-scratchable, un-itchable itching!
But that wasn't all that I would be ditching.
Off went my muscles: no more cramps or aches.
Out went my insides that wiggled like snakes.
Away went my nerves and my tonsils right after;
To be misery free filled me up, up with laughter!

Last were my joints, the biggest offender,
So I picked up a stick that was long, strong, and slender,
And
        WHACK!
                To my knees, to my elbows and back.
        WHACK!
                To my shoulders-

Then I heard a crack.

"What happened then?" the little boy wondered."
The skull said, "It turns out that I'd made a blunder."

I was desperate for relief
But even I should have known
That without skin and muscles
      I was nothing but bones.

My skeleton fell apart
Into a neat little pile
And my skinless little skull
Could do nothing but smile.

Do I regret my decision?
      Maybe a little, it's true,
But I still thinks it's better
Than being sick with the flu.

The little boy nodded
And set the skull down.
He said, "Thanks for the story,"
Then turned right around
      And marched back to his house
         And called to be seen
            By a doctor right then
               For a seasonal vaccine.

ACKNOWLEDGEMENTS

The Caldwell Idaho Writers Group would like to heap lavish praise and thanks upon all the authors who contributed their works to this first anthology, as well as Angela Matlashevsky for her extraordinary book planning, formatting, and design skills; Amy Perry and Ken Nelson, co-owners of the famed Rubaiyat used bookstore, for their gracious hosting; author Neil James for contributing the title story, *The Table by the Window*; Michael T. Smith for sharing his nationally published stories and keen insights into the writing craft; Dylan Cumpton for his tireless editing work; Stacia Perry, group co-chair, for her leadership, planning, and amazing cat-herding abilities, and, finally, Alyssa Cumpton for her marvelous western-noir themed book cover.